AMERICAN LEGIONNAIRE

Amid the burning sands of the desert, the French Foreign Legion is constructing a new fort at Vateau — deep in the territory of El Dowla, ruthless leader of the Bormones, in constant struggle with France for control of the region. He aims to strike hard at the half-built stronghold before it is finished. Meanwhile, among the legionnaires sent out to protect Vateau is an American named Dice Regan — who has a very personal score to settle with El Dowla . . .

Books by John Robb
in the Linford Mystery Library:

JAILBREAK
NO GOLD FOR TINA
FOUR CORPSES IN A MILLION
THE LAST DESERTER
THE BIG HEIST
I SHALL AVENGE!
WE — THE CONDEMNED
ZONE ZERO
MISSION OF MERCY
STORM EVIL

JOHN ROBB

◆

AMERICAN LEGIONNAIRE

Complete and Unabridged

LINFORD
Leicester

First published in Great Britain

First Linford Edition
published 2018

A catalogue record for this book is available
from the British Library.

ISBN 978–1–4448–3948–7

Published by
F. A. Thorpe (Publishing)
Anstey, Leicestershire

Set by Words & Graphics Ltd.
Anstey, Leicestershire
Printed and bound in Great Britain by
T. J. International Ltd., Padstow, Cornwall

This book is printed on acid-free paper

1

To War

For days grim-faced Arabs had been gathering at Haratzo. They came from the south, wherein stood the rich merchant town of Alleto. They came, too, from the desert towns of the north and the east. From every part of Bormone territory they had concentrated on Haratzo for the meeting with El Dowla.

And now, in the conference room of El Dowla's headquarters, the forty-three chieftains squatted upon the cushions and listened while their supreme ruler, the Chosen of Allah, stood in their midst making his final plea.

None could judge the effect which El Dowla's words were having. His audience watched his tall, fat, richly brocaded figure without a flicker of expression.

Every few moments El Dowla's hands would stretch forth from under his silken robes, sometimes in a gesture of fury, sometimes to express persuasion.

' . . . my brethren, I know we have had our setbacks in the past,' he was saying. 'No one has suffered more from them than me. Several times the mostly carefully conceived and executed plans have been broken asunder because of the intervention of the cursed Foreign Legion. But that has been their good fortune — and good fortune does not last any longer than bad. This time . . . we cannot, we shall not, fail. With the building of the new French fort, failure would mean the end of all hope of our independence.'

El Dowla paused, and there was a hint of anxiety in the folds of his fleshy face as he gazed upon his audience. There was good reason for that anxiety. Three times in recent years he had promised them success against the French, and on each occasion there had followed disaster for the Bormones.

He knew that there were whisperings among his people. In the cafés, in the hovels and in the rich men's houses, they were suggesting that the struggle against

2

France was hopeless.

Now he used each trick of mental agility which a western education had taught him in order to stimulate a flagging enthusiasm.

An elderly chieftain unfolded his arms and slowly rose to his feet. The dry, blistering sun rays were shafting through a latticed window and falling directly upon his grey-bearded face. The intense light also reflected from the marble columns and gave even greater brightness to the floor carpets and wall tapestries.

'The Serene El Dowla speaks well of the new fort,' he said in a voice which already held the first croaking intonation of old age. 'We all know that the French started to build it a few weeks ago, and that they are paying for Arab labour. We know, too, that the fort is to be well inside our territory — deeper even than Fort Ney, which has been the furthest the Legion dare to venture. But is this reason enough for a new war against the French? Have we not already tasted sufficient of the battle qualities of the Legion? I urge upon all . . . '

El Dowla broke into his words of caution.

'You ask if the fort is reason enough! How can you doubt it? They are calling it Fort Vateau, and when it is finished it will be as a knife pressed against the throat of the Bormone people. Then there will be no question of resisting the French, for such resistance would be impossible. The time to strike is now, my friends, when little more than the foundations have been laid.'

The elderly Arab had remained standing during El Dowla's interruption. He continued as though the sequence of his words had never been broken.

' . . . we need a long period of peace if our people are to know happiness. Our righteous aspirations must be forgotten — for the time being, at least. It is surely better that we learn to live with the French, to benefit from all that they would offer us.'

El Dowla's normally fat lips had become thin and compressed as the Bormone resumed his place upon the cushions.

'Live in peace with the French! You know not what you say! Are these not our lands, and are they not here as conquerors? Has our race not known a thousand years of martial greatness, and are we to stain that fame now because we have become timid and afraid?

'I hear words about what the French can offer us. They offer only a sham culture, a weakness which they describe as freedom, all of which would result in the decline of the Bormones.'

There was a rustle of robes as several of the chieftains eased their positions, and a muffled sound of agreement. El Dowla's dark eyes held a vivid, strange glitter as he again looked around him.

'But enough of talk. This time, I pledge there will be no failure, for if we fail we die. If each of you gives his forces to my command, then I shall have three times three thousand men. Never before have I had so many. But they will be needed if we are to be saved. That is why I called you together . . . Now, let me know how many stand with me.'

El Dowla pulled on the cord of a wall

bell. Two servants entered. Each bore a shallow enamelled bowl. One was blue, the other red. These were placed side by side on a pile of cushions. El Dowla turned away, staring through the latticed window. Deliberately, he did not look as each of the chieftains tore a short piece from the hem of his robe and placed it in one or other of the bowls.

When all had done, El Dowla turned round. A glance in the vessels was enough. His face stretched into a grim, slightly tired, smile. He counted the strips of linen. Thirty-eight of them came out of the red bowl, only five from the other.

'My people are ready for war,' he said.

★　★　★

Legionnaire Dice Regan savoured the sweet sickliness of his cheap wine, swallowed it, then said: 'So tomorrow we hike over to where they're building Fort Vateau, eh . . . How long's it going to be before that place is finished?'

Glass O'Rane took out his artificial left eye, polished it against the sleeve of his tunic, then reinserted the orb in its socket.

'It takes one helluva a time to build a fort in the desert,' Glass said. 'Particularly a fort that's as far out as that place's going to be. They've only just started on it, and Arab labour doesn't work so fast. I heard it'll take all of another month before even the bare walls and ramparts are up.'

Dice looked dismally round the small, dimly lit café. He groaned, then cursed mildly.

'That means we'll be out there for at least four weeks. Hell — it's always Number One Company that seems to get the no-good work in this man's army.'

Dice was not drunk. It took more wine than any legionnaire could possibly afford to put Dice in that condition. But he was slightly mellowed, a little inclined towards the regretful and the sentimental. It was the way alcohol often affects intelligent and decisive men. He glanced towards the massive figure of Curls Brennan, the third American of the party.

'The prospect doesn't seem to be

troubling you,' he said to Curls. 'Maybe you're figuring on sending us all scatty in the desert with your stories about the time Joe Louis licked the silk pants off you.'

Curls removed his cap for a moment in order to wipe the sweat off the hairless dome of his head. Then he eased his position in his chair. It was like the slow shifting of a bull elephant. He did not look pleased. Once, many years before, Curls had earned a living in the States with his fists. During that period he had boxed an exhibition bout with Joe Louis. He liked to talk about that ring engagement, but he was sensitive about it.

'Joe never licked my pants off. Maybe I haven't told you before, but after that fight Joe said to me . . . '

'You've told us,' Glass said in a firm voice. 'You told us about what Joe Louis said so often that most of us in the company could repeat it all backwards . . . but I'm thinking that after we've been a few weeks in the desert, we'll be so dammed bored we might even be glad to hear your stories again.'

8

Dice called to an Arab waiter and ordered more wine.

There was still half an hour to go before they were due to go out into the narrow streets and alleys of Dini Sadazi and make their way back to barracks. The next morning they would be on the march. On the march to the place where the new fort was going up, deep in Bormone territory. It would be their last night of relaxation for a long, long time. Dice thought they might as well make the most of it.

While waiting for the wine to arrive, he brooded about Dini Sadazi.

It was a funny thing, but you cursed about this little Arab town when you were in it. You cursed it for its heat, for its stinks, for the shadow of the Legion barracks which were always cast over it. But when you came to leave it for a march into the desert, then — well, then things became different. You suddenly found that you kind of liked Dini Sadazi. Found that you didn't much mind the formal discipline which went along with serving in a battalion headquarters.

Maybe you even found that you could tolerate Sergeant Duparne, because Duparne was a bit better when he was stationed in a town than when in the desert or a fort —

Dice's brain revolved moodily, and his eyes were fixed in an unseeing way upon a group of Arab traders haggling over the day's business at a table near the entrance. But suddenly he became aware that someone he knew well had come in the café. Someone he liked, too. It was Phil Marleigh, the English legionnaire of No. 1 Company.

Marleigh seated himself at their table.

Dice poured him a measure of wine, but Marleigh did not drink it immediately. He looked edgy, in the way of a man who is trying to hold down excitement and anxiety. Dice noted the symptoms. They were especially obvious because the Englishman belonged to that category which regards any show of emotion as a weakness.

Dice said: 'Come clean. You've got something to tell us. What is it? We're all listening.'

Marleigh unfastened the top two buttons of his tunic. He answered it in the clipped accent of an English public school.

'It's about Fort Vateau — the place they're building. Because we're due to start for there tomorrow, I thought I'd use the last night in Sadazi by writing a few letters.

'Twenty minutes ago I took them into the company office for censoring. Captain Monclaire was in there, and he was talking about the new fort. It seems there's trouble out there.'

Marleigh paused to take a pull at his wine. He drank the dark fluid greedily, as though he had only just realised how much he wanted it.

Glass hitched his chair closer to the table. He said: 'I hope you've heard wrong. We've had a bellyful of trouble.'

'Unfortunately, I did not hear wrong. I heard Monclaire say that some of the Arabs are refusing to work on the fort. They're quitting every day. Replacements are coming along, but they are getting fewer because it seems that quite a lot of

11

them get cut up by Bormone troops before they get anywhere near Fort Vateau.'

Dice asked: 'Why are the Arabs quitting?'

'Fear. They are scared stiff of what El Dowla's men will do to them if they go on with the work.'

'But they are protected. There are two companies already out there, and we're due to make a third.'

'I know. But from what I can gather, the Arab labourers are not exactly convinced that we can save their hides. You see, there are rumours that El Dowla is trying to mass support from every Bormone chieftain in his territory. Up till now he's always fought with his private army. But if he succeeds in getting backing from the others, well — I don't like to think about what may happen.'

There were a few moments of deep, thoughtful silence. Under the new mental stimulus Dice's head was already clear of drink fumes. His quick, agile brain was probing and analysing the situation. Two years of hard, harsh, automatic Legion discipline had not dulled the sharpness of his mind. On several occasions it had been due to the very quickness of that mind that those round the table were still alive.

Dice broke the quiet. 'I guess something like this was bound to happen.'

Glass looked at him curiously with his single good eye.

'Why? I should have thought that El Dowla had taken enough lickings. It beats me that that fellow doesn't give up his notions about Bormone independence. He's tried hard enough for them, and all they've brought has been plenty of bloodshed and misery.'

Dice fished a half-smoked cigarette from his tunic pocket. In another pocket he found a single match. When the cigarette was alight and he had drawn the first puff deep into his lungs, he said, 'El Dowla's a fiend and a genius. That's a mighty dangerous combination in any man, but particularly so when the man has control over thousands of other humans.

'He really is alight with his ideas of

independence, although anyone with the slightest knowledge of what goes on knows that if the French were to quit his part of Morocco, his rule would be one of the worst tyrannies this part of Africa has known.

'I know he's taken some beatings in the past. But that won't put off a man like him. He's going to war. When a nation or a tribe go to war, they don't do so with the idea that they are going to lose. This was bound to happen, because when Fort Vateau is completed, El Dowla will be completely washed up. The fort would put a Legion force right into the heart of his territory. Every move of his would be under observation.

'Don't you see — somehow, he's got to stop the fort going up. The best way is to put the fear of hell in the people who are building it — the Arabs.'

There was another silence when Dice finished his summing-up. It was a respectful silence.

Glass said: 'When you put things like that, I sort of wonder what the hell you're doing in the Legion.'

It was a quietly spoken, sincere compliment and enquiry. Dice grinned at the compliment, ignored the enquiry. The reason why he'd enlisted was a secret — a secret between himself and another man who was also in Morocco.

'It's a question of knowing how to talk,' Dice said, still smiling. 'It doesn't much matter in this world whether a guy's right or wrong in what he says. It's the way he says it that counts.'

The old bantering, slightly facetious tone had entered his voice. Glass and Marleigh knew it for what it was. It was the pose of a man who wanted to disguise his real, serious personality. They knew it was the reason why Dice showed such an apparent liking for gambling. He'd been named Dice within a few days of appearing at the recruit training depot in Algiers because of his skill in games of chance.

It was the reason why he now produced a pack of playing cards and fanned them out with an expert flick of two fingers.

'How's about a nice game? We've got all of twenty minutes before roll call.'

They drew their chairs closer to the table. They watched Dice shuffle and deal the cards.

But only Curls had nothing on his mind. That was the advantage of being like Curls and not having much under your skull. Men like him do not worry, because they haven't anything to worry with. Still, you don't need a lot of brain when you carry Curls' sort of muscle power around.

But Dice, Glass and Marleigh had quite a lot on *their* minds. They had come up against the Bormones before — too often. In the past they had been lucky. They wondered whether they would be lucky again.

2

Death of the Innocents

In some armies they sing while on the march. Voices rise and fall in harmony with the tramp of feet. It sounds good and it looks good. But they don't do that in the Legion. In that army they've nothing to sing about. And even if they had, it would be difficult to find a song which is common to all of a score or more nationalities. In any case, you need your breath for something more important than lyrics when the sand is tugging at your boots so that your legs are one long ache, and when the Sahara sun is cutting through your flesh and grilling the soft marrow of your bones.

Yet it would be untrue to say that on this, the afternoon of their second day out of Dini Sadazi, No. 1 Company marched in complete silence. There were sounds to be heard. The hollow, slightly unreal tinkling of martial equipment broke the stillness of the desert. So did the heavy breathing of the one hundred and twenty men as they moved three abreast, all bent forward under the weight of their shoulder packs.

As was usual, Dice, Glass, and Curls had got themselves into one file with Dice in the middle. Marleigh was in the file directly behind them. Dice's left hand was pulling forward the sling of his Lebel rifle in an attempt to ease the biting strain on his shoulder. In his other hand he held a piece of rag with which he constantly wiped a sweat-greased face.

He said to no one in particular: 'I'll be darned pleased when we camp for the night . . . I'm just about done in already . . . '

After a few seconds, Glass grunted. Glass was a veteran. He had served for more than four years. It was during those years that he had had an eye shot out. But he still remained one of the best (some said the very best) rifle shots in the Legion. 'The first day's always the worst,' he told Dice. 'After that, you go kind of numb.'

'I know it,' Dice said. 'It's waiting for the numbness to set in that's the rough part.'

'This ain't exactly a tough march. We'll be at Fort Ney tomorrow. We'll be resting up there a while before pushing on to where they're building Fort Vateau.'

Dice did not reply. He was thinking gloomily about Fort Vateau. That was situated on the oasis well to the east of Ney. There would be no proper billets there. They'd be sleeping under canvas — if they were lucky. Most likely they'd have no cover at all. It was a hell of a prospect. And the chance of trouble with the Bormones did not improve it.

At the head of the column, Captain Monclaire was thinking too.

He was thinking about the intelligence reports which had been shown to him before they left Sadazi. Those reports made unsatisfactory reading. It appeared that El Dowla was attempting to mobilise the forces of all the Bormone sub-chieftains under his command. It was not yet clear whether he had achieved this, but if he had — if he had —

Monclaire's imagination was appalled at the prospect. Hitherto, El Dowla's forces had comprised only those raised and equipped directly by himself. Even so, they had been formidable enough. Once, they had even succeeded in temporarily capturing Fort Ney and massacring the garrison. But with the support of the entire race of Bormone warriors spread over thousands of square miles of Morocco . . .

The intelligence department had, of course, been optimistic. They said that El Dowla was not likely to get that support, therefore the addition of a single company to protect the building of Fort Vateau would be enough.

Monclaire was not so certain.

He knew El Dowla. He knew the man's genius as well as his despotism. His gift of leadership, his innate cunning. Faced with such a desperate situation as the building of a Legion base deep in his territory, El Dowla would almost certainly be driven to desperate counter-measures.

Sergeant Duparne was at his side.

Monclaire had discussed the report with Duparne the previous night in the company office, considering it desirable to do so, since the tough little N.C.O. was his immediate subordinate. He wanted to speak about it again. It might relieve his feelings of tension and foreboding.

'I don't expect we'll see much of the Bormones until we're well east of Fort Ney.'

It was more of a search for reassurance than a flat statement of opinion. But Duparne shook his head.

'*Mon capitaine*, I think it possible that the Bormones will try to stop us long before we are anywhere near Vateau. They might well appear before we reach Fort Ney.'

Monclaire was only half-listening. His eyes were fixed on a point some two miles ahead and several degrees to the north.

Something was dimming the deep and vivid blue of the sky. Something seemed to rise out of the sand, and shimmer faintly yet darkly toward the heavens. Suddenly Monclaire knew what it was. It was smoke.

But smoke in the desert with the sun still at great strength . . .

No one but a madman would light a fire under such circumstances.

He touched Duparne's elbow, but the sergeant was already looking. For a time he was as stupefied as Monclaire. Then he said quietly, 'That is about the direction of the village of Karak, *mon officier*.'

Monclaire said a single word to the sergeant. A second later Duparne's shrill voice cut through the hot air.

'*Halt!*' Because the order was unexpected, some of the legionnaires stumbled on for a pace or two, and the whole company came to a shambling stop.

Monclaire groped for his map-case and withdrew a long role of thick linen paper. Duparne held one side of it while the company officer checked their position. Then he said: 'You are right. That will be Karak. It is marked here as a small Arab settlement round a seasonal oasis. But I can't recall ever being there.'

'I have visited it many years ago, *mon capitaine*. It was typical. A hundred or two Arabs in it, no more.'

Monclaire stroked his thin black moustache.

'We'll have to make a small detour and visit Karak. It may be nothing, but *ma foi*, I cannot understand it. It looks as though it is the smoke from a fire which is almost dead . . . a very big fire.'

Duparne gave a second order. '*En avant!*' The company moved again, this time in the direction of Karak.

Death — particularly recent death — can have a greater effect upon the nerves than anything within the power of the living. It can, for example, be sensed long before it is seen. In this respect, human beings have a lot in common with other animals. A dog or a horse can put back its head and know that many miles away one of its kind had died. So can a man. Not in city streets, perhaps. But certainly in the lonely and the primitive places. In the desert, for example.

Thus every soldier in the company somehow knew what he would see long before he was within sight of Karak.

It was not a matter of deduction from the faint and fading cloud of smoke. It was a matter of innate instinct.

They knew that they would march into a pathetic mound of smouldering chattels which had until a short time ago been the equipment of the Arab hovels. They knew they would see in each of the short alleys the inert ugliness of people who had died suddenly and horribly. Yet their fore-knowledge did not soften the shock when it was offered to their eyes.

When they halted in the midst of what had been the Arab settlement of Karak, a shuddering breath of revulsion ran along the line of the company. It was followed by a few seconds of abject quiet, as though the living were sharing the stillness of the dead. Then there was a muffled burst of indignation — indigna-tion which was expressed in many tongues.

Dice said in a strained, croaking way: 'Only fiends could have done this — '

And Glass answered: 'Only El Dowla's Bormones could have done it.'

Outside each of the mud hovels and beside the charred remnants of tents, the dead were lying.

There had been no mercy, not a vestige of discrimination. Women and children had been cut down in common with the men. And on some of their faces the dying expression of horror still remained. Already flies were gathered thickly over the fresh and gaping scimitar cuts.

It had been a massacre of a defenceless village. The butchers of hell had been through Karak.

Marleigh phrased the question which was going through everyone's mind.

'But why — why? There's no sense in this. The Bormones must have done it — those wounds could only have been made by their scimitars. Yet why should they do it to a peaceful village?'

'I figure we'll never know,' Glass said. 'There's no one left alive here. It's been a thorough job of work.'

But his statement was disproved the same minute it was uttered.

There was a movement among a group of five bodies which lay outside one of the hovels. It was a very faint movement, but in the absolute stillness it was immediately obvious to the entire company. The eyes of every legionnaire were instantly fixed upon the spot. They saw the scraggy brown arm flicker a few inches upwards, then subside as though exhausted with the effort.

Monclaire and Duparne moved quickly towards it. The flies buzzed reluctantly away as they bent over the sprawled bodies. They moved two of them aside and revealed an old Arab who wore a straggly, blood-soaked beard.

A sword slash had sunk deep into one taut, crinkled cheek, and his soiled and greasy robes showed a big red patch from a wound across his chest. It needed only a quick examination to show that he had not long to live.

Monclaire uncorked his water bottle. Cushioning the Arab's head on one arm, he forced some of the liquid down his throat. The aged eyes flickered open. They had the dark flatness of one who is about to pass through the abyss. There was no expression there. Not fear, not surprise. And his breath was coming so slowly as to be nearly undetectable.

Very gently, Monclaire said in Arabic:

'Did the Bormone warriors do this?'

There was a long interval during which it seemed as though the question had not been understood. Then, at last, the Arab nodded his head. But he did not attempt to speak.

Monclaire continued: 'Why was it done?'

Again there was the pause. The old man seemed to be gathering himself for the effort of words. When those words came they were in no more than a quavering whisper.

'We sent . . . we sent men to aid in the — building of the fort at Vateau — El Dowla told us not to do this, but our young men did not listen . . . he is to do this to all villages who help the Legion . . . thus is the vengeance of El Dowla . . . the . . . '

He died before the faltering sentence could be finished.

Monclaire lowered his head and stood upright. His lips were drawn tight and he looked heavy with weariness as he glanced first at Duparne, then at the column of legionnaires who were standing at ease, most of them resting on the butts of their rifles.

It was as he had expected, as he had feared. El Dowla would not dare to use such methods of primitive terror if he had not the support of all the Bormone chieftains. Therefore it seemed he had achieved his aim of gathering under his command forces which had never before been equalled by an insurgent . . .

The intelligence department had been wrong in their forecast. It was a peculiar thing about the intelligence department, Monclaire thought, that though they did excellent work in gathering facts, they were usually inaccurate when they tried to make deductions from them.

'The dead must be buried immediately,' he told Duparne, 'or the vultures will have them. It is only the fire and smoke which has kept them away until now. After that is done — I think we may have to change our plans.'

Duparne was too old a soldier to enquire into what the change might be. Instead, he bawled out a series of orders; and within a few minutes the entire company, except for a small picket, was at work digging a mass grave with their short entrenching tools.

By now the sun was well down and the worst of the heat was over. Monclaire moved a little way out of the precincts of the dead village and again fumbled with his map case. He sat on the sand and unrolled the paper. He wanted to study that map and think.

The Arab had said that El Dowla had threatened to massacre all other villages which sent labour to Vateau . . .

Which would he be likely to attack next in his reign of terror? The nearest place was Balati. This was larger than Karak. According to his map reference it had a population of about a thousand. It was only fourteen miles due east. And Balati, he knew, had supplied men for Fort Vateau.

Balati was as likely as any to be the next — if it had not already been attacked.

It was at this point that Monclaire faced the problem which at some time confronts every soldier. It was the problem of whether he was justified in acting on his own initiative.

His orders, given to him before leaving Dini Sadazi, had been clear enough. He was to proceed to Port Ney, which was commanded by Major Dux, rest his men there for one day, then continue the march on to Vateau.

But those orders took no account of this development. Should he take a gamble and move first on Balati in the hope of being there when the Bormones attacked the village — *if* they attacked the village?

There was little doubt that if he were able to stop another massacre, he would be judged correct in taking such an action. But if, on the other hand, he waited for days at Balati for an attack which did not materialise . . . He shuddered at the prospect. He might even be court-martialled for disobeying orders.

Mentally, Monclaire resolved the problem in this way: If he *did* go to Balati and there was *not* an attack, he would be in trouble. But if he did *not* go to Balati and there *was* an attack, he would also be in trouble. *Mon Dieu*, but the odds were weighed in favour of misfortune!

As he folded the map, Monclaire made up his mind. He strode back to Duparne, who was now supervising the filling of the grave.

He raised his cane in an answering salute as Duparne clicked to attention.

'*Mon sergent*,' he said, 'we're going to Balati.'

3

Balati

An almost full moon was riding fast and high over the desert when they approached Balati.

The village lay in a declivity, and they first saw it as a sprawling mass of substance and shadow. Duparne gave the order to halt in an unusually quiet voice, but the company obeyed it without hesitation. Each man understood the necessity for silence at this time.

Dice watched Monclaire survey the distant village through his field glasses. He turned and whispered to Marleigh: 'It doesn't look as if this place's been visited by the Bormones.'

Marleigh nodded and shivered slightly. They had all been oozing sweat a few hours before. Now, in the comparative night cold, they had sunk their chins under the upturned collars of their tunics.

'From what Monclaire's told us, Balati is quite likely to be in trouble before long,' he said.

Before leaving Karak, Monclaire had explained briefly to the company the reasons for his change of plan. It was not his habit to justify his orders before the legionnaires, but like all good officers, Monclaire was able to recognise the times when all ranks must know the reasons behind decisions. Such occasions were exceptional, but they occurred.

Glass said: 'There isn't a Bormone soldier inside of ten miles from here — if there were, I'd smell them.'

It was not an altogether idle boast. Glass, like many veteran campaigners, had an instinct when it came to sensing the presence of an enemy.

'They are not likely to be around now,' Dice told him. 'The Bormones don't usually make trouble at night.'

Balati was sleeping when they entered the outskirts of the village. But it did not sleep for long after that. Although the entrance was made with as much silence as is possible for a hundred and twenty men in full equipment, it created enough sound to rouse the inhabitants.

At first, a few bleary and dirty heads jutted out from the mud hovels and blinked with astonishment at the marching column. More heads appeared, and gradually whole bodies emerged into the narrow, dirty streets, and converged on the market square where the company halted. Within a few minutes a tight-packed crowd had formed a circle round them. The air buzzed with Arabic conjecture and opinion. Women held their children up, and many of those at the back thrust and scuffled so as to get a better view of the unexpected arrivals.

It was noticeable that there were not many young men among the crowd. Most of them had volunteered for work on the new fort.

There was a sudden silence when Monclaire held up his hands as an indication that he was about to speak to them.

Monclaire's Arabic was fairly fluent. In crisp, clear tones he told them that the village was in danger from the warriors of El Dowla, and the Legion had arrived as friends to protect them. He asked that food be supplied to the legionnaires.

He did not enter into details. He confined his message to a few simple sentences. They were received in silence — the sort of silence that can be felt. Hundreds of dark, thin faces were regarding him with a mixture of incredulity and faint hostility.

It was obvious that the traditional Arab suspicion had been stirred. Monclaire was well aware of that. He was about to speak again when an elderly man in a greasy robe pushed out of the throng. He leaned on a palm stick as he moved slowly towards Monclaire. He stopped within a few feet of him. When he spoke, it became apparent that he carried authority in the village. His voice emerged from his beard with clipped precision.

'You speak to us of danger from the warriors of El Dowla,' he said. 'But why should we be in danger from him? We know that he is your enemy and you have fought many battles. But we do not know that he is an enemy of peaceful Arabs such as dwell in Balati.'

There was a rumble of agreement from around him. The man had summed up the opinion of the village.

Monclaire said evenly: 'We can speak better if I know your name.'

'I am Bel Hassal and I speak for the people of this place.'

Monclaire nodded at him.

'Then you will know, Bel Hassal, that many of your young men have left here to build our new fort.'

'I do. This is but a poor place, and the money the French are paying is riches indeed to us.'

'Do you know that El Dowla is trying to prevent the fort being built?'

'That may well be so — but it is no concern of ours.'

'It is your concern, *mon ami*. We have just left the village of Karak, and there is not a person left alive in it. They were massacred by the Bormones, and there could be only one reason — because they were helping the Legion . . . '

Bel Hassal raised a shaking hand to his forehead and blinked with dim eyes at Monclaire.

'All the people of Karak dead . . . killed by the Bormones! If I did not know that French officers do not lie . . . '

He was mentally reeling under the impact. Monclaire drove home his point.

'That is why we are here. We wish to save your people from the same fate, for why should you receive more mercy from El Dowla than the people of Karak? But we must have your aid. My men are weary. They need food and a place to rest.'

Bel Hassal hesitated only long enough to glance at the people he led. That single glance was enough. The suggestion of hostility to the legionnaires had now disappeared. Instead, they all bore the vacant expressions of those who suddenly fear for their lives.

'You shall have the aid of the people of Balati,' he said simply. 'Our food is yours, and a score of our homes shall be emptied so that your soldiers may sleep.'

Monclaire inclined his head in a silent gesture of understanding. Then he said: 'That is well. Your people will be paid for the food and shelter.'

There were some protests, though they were not very strong ones, when twenty families were ordered out of their hovels and told to share other dwellings.

Two-thirds of the company were granted a rest period. The others were placed at strategic guard points round the village.

Dice and Marleigh were put in one of the hovels, while Glass and Curls were among the men who took the first guard duty.

There was no room to stand in that hovel. In fact, the ceiling was so low that it was only just possible to sit upright in it. The place measured no more than six feet by four. In the narrow confines a stink of stale food and staler bodies seemed to have taken the place of air. There was no lamp, but a faint illumination came from the moon which beamed through the low entrance.

They threw themselves on the mud floor. Sheepskins were available as coverings, but they did not use them. They were almost certainly verminous. Marleigh felt in his breast pocket and pulled out a cigarette case. No one in the company, not even Dice, had had the opportunity of examining that case at close quarters. But they knew it was of silver and it had a crest of some sort engraved upon it. Marleigh was the only legionnaire who possessed such a case. Obviously it was a link with his home — with England. No one questioned him about it. They each took a cigarette and smoked slowly, their heads pillowed on their shoulder packs.

After a while, Dice said: 'You know . . . I have a funny kind of feeling. It's difficult to explain, but it's as if something big is going to start happening. Not just an attack by the Bormones, but something a helluva lot more important than that . . . '

The lighted end of Marleigh's cigarette moved up and down as he nodded agreement.

'That's just the way I feel, too. Perhaps we're both a bit scared. We've come across the Bormones often before, and we've had a lot of luck. At the back of our minds we may be wondering whether that luck is going to hold.'

Dice stubbed out his cigarette and pocketed the half-smoked remains.

'I guess it's something like that. But this must be El Dowla's last throw, and I've a hunch that this time he'll either destroy us for good, or we'll finish him. There'll be no half-measures.'

He closed his eyes and within a few minutes was asleep.

★   ★   ★

Two hours after dawn, the heat of the sun was beginning to mount towards its searing crescendo. It flamed down on a silent, waiting village. Balati was encircled by a thin line of legionnaires. They were concealed behind the mud buildings or in quickly dug foxholes. Behind them and watching them, the inhabitants stood in uneasy knots, talking only in whispers. The eyes of everyone were constantly traversing the shimmering undulations of the desert.

Since the first light there had been nothing to see out there — nothing except the occasional expectant flight of a vulture.

Dice and Marleigh had been posted at the easterly side of the village. They were crouched under the cover of a disused and rotting hovel. A few yards to their right, Glass and Curls were lying on either side of an empty Arab tent. All were fingering their Lebels. The butts and breech blocks were smeared with sweat from nervous hands.

Dice glanced at the sun, noted its position, and said: 'If anything's going to happen we ought to see the first signs of it soon. If we don't see any Bormones by mid-day, I guess we'll have been wasting our time.'

'You're probably right,' Marleigh answered. 'Since some of El Dowla's men are in this neighbourhood, they're most likely to visit this place early — if they're going to visit it at all. But the way . . . '

His voice faded out. At the same time Dice ceased to listen. Both of them were watching a patch of the desert which was on the horizon. There was a suggestion of movement there, like the flickering of shadows. It was nothing more. Nothing substantial, nothing which could be defined.

But gradually, very gradually, the shadows hardened and became larger as they approached Balati. When they were a mile away there was no further doubt. They were Bormone cavalry. There were between forty and fifty of them.

From the centre of the village there sounded a short whistle blast. It came from Monclaire. In answer to the pre-arranged order, every safety catch was pressed forward, and all the legionnaires who were facing the horsemen raised their Lebels to their shoulders.

When they were within half a mile, the detail of the Bormones became clear. It was possible to make out the red edging to their white silk robes which splayed backwards as they spurred their horses. It was possible to see their drawn scimitars, the blades pointing forward past the heads of the beasts.

Before another minute had passed, the muffled thunder of the hooves reached their ears, and the hard-set expressions on

42

the warriors' faces could be discerned. They were bunched close together in deep formation.

Dice said: 'This is going to be perfect . . . when we open up, not one of those thugs is going to survive.'

Dice would have been right, had it not been for the jitters of a certain Legionnaire Stamm.

The Bormones did not at first suspect danger. They were charging in for a quick, ruthless orgy of death in the village. A dozen experienced riflemen could have disposed of them. Ten times that number were available.

They were awaiting the second blast from Monclaire's whistle. That would be the signal to open fire. They knew it would not be given until the last possible moment. Monclaire would wait until the Bormones were almost at sword-thrust range before releasing a whining curtain of lead into their midst. In this way, he would ensure that a single first volley would finish the career of every horseman.

That was Monclaire's plan — but

Legionnaire Stamm wrecked it.

Stamm was one of nature's petty cruelties. He was a man who was doomed to stumble through life saying and doing the wrong thing. He also looked wrong — looked ridiculous. The little Dutchman had an enormous belly which drooped down towards his thin knees. He had a pink round face which bore a perpetually anxious aspect. He was that unfortunate sort of man who can never do anything right.

Stamm had been posted at the corner of an alley. From this position he had a superb view of the approaching cavalry, for they were bearing down directly on the point at which he was standing trembling.

When he heard the first whistle, Stamm realised that it was the signal to sight rifles. He raised his Lebel to his shoulder and blinked along the barrel. Suddenly he felt an acute flash of doubt. Had he remembered to load the magazine? That should have been done two hours ago, when they took up their defensive positions. Stamm was almost certain that he had forgotten . . .

He felt a new burst of sweat stream down his face. The Bormones only a few hundred yards away, and he was standing here with an empty rifle! He just had time to get a clip in the magazine. Even now, his personal panic need have caused no trouble if he had drawn back the bolt in the normal manner. But Stamm did not do that. Stamm pressed the trigger so as to release the cocked firing pin.

The Lebel nudged his thin shoulder and a whip-like report echoed through Balati and across the desert.

If Stamm had been deliberately aiming at anything it would have been an excellent shot. But he was not even looking through his sights at the time. The bullet which entered the chest of one of the leading Bormones, and caused him to fall sideways off the saddle and under the following hooves, was a complete accident.

The result was a two-fold chaos.

The Bormones began to rein in their foaming steeds, and some of the closely packed animals crashed into each other.

The legionnaires were baffled. Most, however, continued to hold their fire. But some, hearing the single shot and concluding that the whistle signal must have been given, opened a few sporadic rounds on the Bormones.

But the range was still too extreme for the fire to be effective. No more than half a dozen horses and men had been hit when the Bormones turned and galloped back into the desert.

Monclaire cursed. He knew exactly what had happened, though he did not yet know who had fired the accidental shot. He was about to raise the whistle to his lips when he abruptly changed his mind. Already the cavalry were a good half-mile away. To try to pursue them with lead would be foolish and ineffective.

His brow was dark as he snapped at Duparne: 'Find who discharged that shot. The man is to be brought to me immediately.'

Duparne saluted.

'*Oui, mon capitaine*, but I fear it will be difficult.'

Monclaire rubbed his rough, dark chin.

He realised that the culprit would be most unlikely to declare himself, and it would be impossible to prove who it was.

'Very well. The order is countermanded. The damage is done and nothing can undo it. As you know, it was my hope to kill every one of those Bormones so that their disappearance would be a mystery to El Dowla. *Ma foi*, but now he will know that we are here, and will surely guess that we are on the way to Vateau . . . ' He glanced up at the clear, deep blue sky, and added: 'The storm clouds are gathering, *mon sergent* . . . '

4

The Net

El Dowla had a virtue which is common to all natural leaders of men. He always gave the most precise attention to every report presented to him — no matter how trivial it might appear to be. In that way, he often obtained information of the utmost value. Thus he listened carefully to the story of the weary cavalry officer who stood before him.

The officer's white silk robes were stained with dirt and sand. His hawk-like features were drawn, strained. When he had finished speaking, El Dowla regarded him with curious interest. He gestured towards a crystal wine decanter.

'You may drink,' he said. 'Good wine will lessen your fatigue. So the Legion were in Balati . . . they must be on their way to strengthen the guard at Vateau. I'd suspected that the infidels might do this,

48

and it is good — it is what I want.'

The officer drank the wine greedily and then lowered his head in agreement. He said, 'I do not think there are many of them. There were but few rifles fired upon us, although we adjudged it better to return rather than risk losses in combat.'

'You did well, for the Legion may have been in greater strength than you think. What you tell me does not suggest the usual Legion methods.'

Seeing that the officer looked puzzled, El Dowla went on: 'You say that they first fired a single shot, and this was followed by a ragged volley . . . that is not the way the Legion usually work. They are usurpers in our country, but they are also good soldiers. No, what you tell me makes me think that there was possibly a misunderstanding over orders. They would be waiting until you got very close, but due to an error one of their number fired too soon.'

'Then, my lord Dowla, how many do you think were in the village?'

'A full company, probably. They usually move reinforcements in units of such a size.'

El Dowla had been sitting in a high-backed carved chair. The fact that he favoured this rather than the traditional cushions was a result of his western education. He rose slowly from it. Despite his gross bulk, El Dowla usually contrived to move with forceful dignity. He crossed a few paces towards a low table. On it there was a large wooden frame. The frame was filled with sand of varying depths. And dotted on it were groups of stones. The stones represented towns, villages and Legion forts. It was a crude relief representation of the Bormone area of the Sahara.

For a few moments El Dowla looked down upon it. He ran the tip of his tongue round his thick, copper-hued lips. It was a faintly gloating movement. Indeed, every fleshy line of his face had assumed an aspect of almost salacious satisfaction.

With his index finger he pointed to a single pebble on the sand. The officer drew near, looking at the mark with respectful attention.

'There we have Fort Ney,' El Dowla

said. 'It is certain that the Legion company will even now be on their way there to rest before moving on to Vateau — which is here.'

His finger moved towards another pebble. He went on: 'I propose to make it impossible for that company to reach Vateau. This will be done by confining them in Fort Ney. Now that I have great numbers of warriors at my command, it will be easy. A thousand men will surround that fort, thus none of the men inside it will be able to leave.

'There will be no attempt to storm the place. Because the garrison is now very much larger than before, such an operation would be costly and quite unnecessary. To use a European military term, we will simply seal off the enemy.

'Thus it will be even easier for us to interrupt and eventually prevent the building of the fort at Vateau. Already many Arabs are afraid to volunteer for work there, in spite of the payment the French are offering. When news spreads of what has occurred at Karak, the flow of labour should entirely cease.

'Our next and immediate task is to quicken the rate of desertion among those who are already working there. That, too, will not be difficult. Listen, and you will understand why the dominion of France over our land is almost at an end . . . '

El Dowla's voice purred on, and as he absorbed the information, the officer's hand involuntarily gripped the hilt of his scimitar. The lust for blood was being stirred.

★ ★ ★

Dice knew that he was awake when he realised that he was looking at a thick curtain of vivid red. He was awake, but his eyes were still closed. Slowly, he blinked them open, and the intense sunlight which had been shining through his lids now streamed through the slit windows directly onto his eyeballs.

He yawned, then sat sideways on his bunk. Most of the other legionnaires were already moving slowly about in the barrack room. Some were smoking and talking in small groups. Every few moments, one or two of them would break into laughter as a story was finished — the sort of story which soldiers have laughed at since the start of time. Others were seated round the bare wooden table in the centre of the long room, playing a hand of cards. A few, like Dice, were sitting on the edges of their bunks, concentrating on the process of becoming completely awake.

No. 1 Company had arrived at Fort Ney from Balati five hours before. That had been a couple of hours before mid-day. Since then, they had been sleeping — sleeping away the fatigue of the long desert march from Dini Sadazi. Sleeping, too, so as to escape the worst of the grilling heat which seemed to concentrate on Fort Ney. But in another hour they would have to face that heat.

They would be parading in the open square of the fort for *appel*. With all the rest of the garrison, they would stand at rigid attention while answering the long roll-call.

Glass was fixing in his artificial eye. When he had done that, he sat on Dice's tunic. He, too, was thinking about the coming agony of the *appel*.

'There are times,' Glass said with harsh emphasis, 'when I kind of wonder whether a roll-call is really necessary in a place like this.'

Dice was watching the card game, but he said: 'I guess some guys might desert. It's been known. We once tried it.'

'Sure, so some guys might desert. But just how are they going to get out of a fort? Tell me that. It's fixed up so that an army of Bormones can't get in, so how the hell is an odd soldier going to get out?'

Dice laughed. What Glass said was true enough. *Appel* in Fort Ney was one of those military tortures devised to serve the purpose of discipline. Except, of course, during periods of emergency, the entire garrison excepting the guards slept during the torrid afternoons. Even the Legion recognised that this mercy was vital to the health of the legionnaires. But it was almost as though *appel* was designed to make them pay for the period of rest.

Marleigh joined them. He was rubbing his fair head as though to massage away the remnants of sleep. He said, 'We've got our equipment to clean.'

Dice yawned again.

'You worry too much,' he told him. 'I think maybe I'll take a hand in that game.'

He uncoiled his wiry figure from the bunk and moved to the table. Four men were seated there, each fingering a hand of greasy cards. None of them had any money in front of him. None of them possessed any money. They were playing for their next instalment of pay. They would get that when they returned to Sadazi.

Dice sat himself beside Patruski, the Russian. He watched the hand being played out, then when Patruski took over the deal, Dice received five cards. Within a few moments he was calculating, bluffing, bidding. And he was forgetting — temporarily forgetting. The drug of gambling was dulling the memory of a home he had once known in America. A home where his brother had bid him farewell before setting out on mission work in North Africa.

The chance of the cards was removing from his mind the recollection of that man, younger than Dice, who had always been serious, always responsible. A brother who Dice admired. His imagination was not now being tortured by the memory of the day when he heard that his brother had been murdered by Bormone Arabs — at the direct order of El Dowla, it was said. Under the anaesthetic of the game his mind was rested. Rested from the wild wonderings about the way in which his brother had been killed. Rested from the unwavering desire for vengeance . . .

Marleigh had found a French newspaper. It had been used as padding over the unrelenting wires of his bunk, and it was more than a year old. He went through the process of translating the headlines, but he too was only stifling the figments of the past.

The yellowing newsprint prevented his mind dwelling on the mischances and tragedies which had forced him to leave

England, to leave his friends, and come to this — to this hell-spot of Africa, in association with some of the toughest and worst men on earth . . . as well as some of the best men on earth.

Glass was sitting beside Curls. Curls was flexing his barrel-like biceps as he demonstrated the sort of punches he'd thrown when he met up with Joe Louis. For once, Glass was not bored with the story. He was not bored because he was not listening —

Glass had forgotten why he'd joined the Legion. He'd enlisted a hell of a long time ago, and a guy just can't remember everything. Right now, he was trying to figure out whether he had ten or eleven more months to serve before his time was up.

When his time was up . . .

Glass let his mind play with the prospect. He saw himself in civilian clothes again. In a nice double-breasted coat. He'd get himself a velour hat, too. One of those with a snap down brim . . . but maybe velour hats weren't worn any more. It was a heck of a time since he'd last seen civilians moving around. Fashions could have changed since then.

Although Curls was doing the talking, he was not altogether concentrating on his own words. One half of his mind was wondering whether a guy could still make a living out of the fight game. Sure, he wasn't as young as he had been, but that went for most everyone. Maybe when he got out of this man's army he'd try a comeback in the fight rings of the States. When he got out —

In short, it was one of those times when soldiers are either thinking about the past and the future — or deliberately trying not to think about them.

The atmosphere in that barrack room was typical of the fevered peace before a climax. The storm was near, and already the sound of it was tearing at their subconscious minds —

The storm burst at ten minutes before the time for *appel*.

First warning of it was given by Legionnaire Fryppo.

All that day, Fryppo had been cursing his misfortune. He'd been hoping to escape duty in the watch-tower for at least another week. In fact, if such things were worked out according to the dictates of justice, he should not be on the duty for a fortnight. But it had happened that he'd been checked by his corporal for having dust in the sights of his Lebel. Not a lot of dust, just a grain or two. But it had been enough for his name to be moved forward dramatically on the watch-tower rota. So, for three-hour periods with thirty minutes' rest in between, he'd been up on that two-hundred-foot-high roof since shortly after dawn.

That meant that he'd been there for rather more than twelve hours. Fryppo blinked dismally out across the desert and wondered whether he dare to risk reading that last letter he'd had from his home in Lisbon. That letter had been tempting him all the time he'd been up there. But once again he decided to leave it in his tunic pocket. The penalty if he were seen neglecting watch-tower duty was too horrible even to consider.

Up here, only a few feet below the flapping tricolour of France, he was supposed to keep a constant watch on the entire circumference of the desert. The trouble was that you had to do just that. If you relaxed for too long, some damned officer or N.C.O. would be sure to see you and bawl up from the parade ground far below.

Fryppo raised the field glasses. They were issue field glasses which were kept constantly on the watch-tower for use of the men on duty there. This meant that they were not very good ones. They had been handled by so many clumsy fingers for so many years that the lenses were now out of true.

In fact, from the optical point of view, they were more of a hindrance than a help. They offered to the user an enlarged fuzz of distant objects. But they were useful for giving the impression of alert vigilance. Staring upwards from the parade ground, many an officer had been deceived by the sight of the watch-tower guard sweeping the horizon with his glasses. He was not to know that the instrument made the horizon all but invisible.

It was not surprising, therefore, that at first Legionnaire Fryppo did not observe the white cloud upon the sand.

That was what it appeared to be. A cloud, long and deep, which was moving at ground level in the direction of the fort. It had long since mounted the horizon, and was less than two miles distant when Fryppo finally detected it. He lowered the glasses so as to be able to see it better.

As it drew closer, Fryppo knew that it was no meteorological phenomenon. The whiteness was not the white of water vapour. It was that of flowing robes — of Bormone robes.

Some were mounted on horseback, others were afoot. But all were moving in the direction of the fort. They were moving slowly, and it seemed that the horsemen were travelling no faster than the others. The effect was faintly weird.

A brass alarm bell was slung from a wooden frame at the side of the flagpole. Fryppo was moving towards it when he chanced to glance towards another section of the desert. He took in a deep breath, wiped sweat off his forehead, and cursed.

Another body of Bormones was approaching from the opposite direction to the first. They too totalled several hundred. For a few seconds Legionnaire Fryppo jerked his head from one to another like a confused puppet.

Then he jumped at the alarm bell.

5

The Siege

Dice was holding a nice hand. There were two aces in it. He was about to play one of them when the bell rang.

Marleigh was looking dejectedly at a French crossword puzzle, and wondering how long it would take to solve it, when the bell rang.

Glass was thinking about the day when he'd be free of the Legion. He was trying to figure out whether he'd be able to work his passage back to the States when the bell rang.

Curls was wondering about this guy they called Lee Savold. He was wondering whether he was as tough as Louis when the bell rang.

It was not a musical bell. It was cast with a view to volume rather than tone. It certainly fulfilled the wishes of its designers. When Legionnaire Fryppo struck it with the butt of his Lebel, the resultant noise was like a command of the gods.

It thundered and reverberated through every cranny of Fort Ney. It was so deep and ugly a note that it seemed temporarily to shatter the senses.

When Captain Monclaire heard it, he was in his room looking through a copy of the French Army lists. He was reading gloomily down the columns of names of other men who held the rank of captain, and was trying to estimate just what his prospects of an early promotion were. He had just decided that these prospects were not good when the bell sounded.

Sergeant Duparne was struggling through his thick beard with a semi-blunt razor. The sudden deep, resonant tone resulted in a nasty cut in the centre of his chin.

The orders for such an emergency were so well-known, so often rehearsed, that there was no need for any spoken word of command. Every company, every platoon, every section had its post. They all went to them with the unhurried speed of men who are trained for the task in hand.

Most of them went up the stone steps and took up positions on the platform under the ramparts of the walls. Others went to guard points within the fort. These included the armoury, where the normal guard of two sentries was suddenly increased to twenty, and the magazine, where an addition of thirty sentries brought the strength up to thirty-four.

As soon as the defensive positions were taken up, the fort commandant climbed the vertical iron ladder which reached to the top of the watch-tower.

The commandant was Major Dux.

Major Dux was a tired man. He was tired of being at Fort Ney — which was understandable, for no officer had ever enjoyed a period of being posted there. He was tired of serving in this part of Africa. He wanted a nice headquarters posting where a fellow could live in reasonable comfort. Most of all, he was tired of Arabs.

The major had a small, portly figure. His was the sort of shape which strutted importantly through life, the sort of mentality which basked in its own esteem. He considered himself to be an outstanding military intellect whose enterprise and vision was being woefully wasted. That opinion was not shared among the headquarters staff at Algiers. It was for that reason that he'd been posted to Fort Ney. There, he could not do much harm. The defence of a fort was such a simple matter.

One thing could be said for Major Dux. He was consistent. He was always wrong.

Thus, when he reached the top of the watch-tower, he came to an immediate decision to send an officer out to speak with the leaders of the Bormones. He announced this resolve to Monclaire, who had followed him up the ladder.

Monclaire looked towards the Bormones. They were now within a half-mile of the fort and had formed a circle. Every warrior, whether horseman or on foot, had drawn his scimitar, and the blades were glinting in the afternoon sun. Having summed up the situation, Monclaire gazed with astonishment at Dux.

'*Mon Dieu!* You can't send an officer out to speak with the Bormones . . . he'd never return. Those men have not come here to talk, they are here for war, *mon commandant*. Judging by the way they are grouping, I'd say they intend to lay siege to the fort.'

Major Dux had the usual obstinacy of mediocre men. At the back of his mind he suspected that Monclaire was right — but that made him the more determined to prove this junior officer wrong. He turned an indignant round face on the captain.

'You must permit me to handle this affair in my own way, for I'm not without experience. I consider it most probable that the Bormones have come to clear up some misunderstanding, and it would be criminal not to give them the opportunity of stating their case.'

Monclaire pulled at his moustache. He blinked incredulously at Dux. He'd heard vaguely about Major Dux before, but today had marked their first meeting. He'd heard that Dux was something of a fool, but he'd not paid much attention to that. He'd put it down to normal malicious mess-room gossip. But, *ma foi*! He'd never for a moment imagined that the fellow knew so little about the enemy around him. It was madness that such a man should be in command of a key fort.

'So you think they have come to clear up a misunderstanding! So they have — with bullets and scimitars,' Monclaire said, his voice almost choking as he attempted to control his wrath. 'There must be a thousand of them out there — look, already they are circling the fort! Does that look as if they are here for a conference?'

Dux was aware of a steadily growing distaste for Monclaire. Because of his senior rank, there was no need for him to disguise the fact. This captain had got himself some sort of reputation as a desert fighter. No doubt much of it was exaggerated. But it had certainly gone to his head. He must be put in his place. He must be shown who was in command at Fort Ney.

'I'm not discussing my decision further,' he said briskly. 'You will kindly confine yourself to carrying out my orders, Capitaine Monclaire.'

Monclaire shrugged his shoulders.

'I have no choice, *mon commandant*. But may I suggest that, if you insist on parleying with the Bormones, you invite a few of them into the fort. In that way, you'll not endanger the life of an officer.'

Major Dux raised a plump fist to give emphasis to his answer.

'I shall not. If I send an officer out to meet them, it will have a most profound moral effect. The Bormones will see that we are not afraid.'

'Then I fear that the officer will not come back. It will be murder, *mon commandant*, and in due course it will be my duty to send a report on the matter to the general staff at Algiers.'

Monclaire's voice was clear now, as though all emotion had left him.

For a long couple of seconds Major Dux's lower jaw remained limp and slightly open as the significance of the words stirred his mind.

'You are threatening me, *mon capitaine?*'

'*Non*. It is not a threat, it is a statement of my military duty. If you are right in the action you propose to take, then you have nothing to fear from any report I may make.'

Dux turned his back upon Monclaire and turned his small round eyes towards the Bormones. They had halted now within seven hundred yards of the fort, forming a circle round it. Obviously they were intending to camp in that position, for most of them were putting up small tents and the horses were being tethered together. Although they were slightly beyond accurate small-arms range, several hundred of them had taken up prone firing positions, and their rifles were levelled at the ramparts of the fort.

Suddenly Dux felt a spasm of fear. He'd been lucky up to now. In all his Legion service, he'd never been in a serious action. But he certainly did not like the look of this . . .

His gaze swivelled towards the men, his men, who knelt behind the ramparts. He felt a little reassured. It was a big garrison, and it had been further strengthened by the arrival of Monclaire's company. That swine Monclaire . . .

Major Dux was smiling when he turned

back towards Monclaire. There was an oozing, unhealthy satisfaction about him.

He said: 'You will speak with the Bormones. You will be the officer to approach them, *capitaine* — '

Monclaire pursed his lips. He started to whistle softly. He whistled the opening bars of Pasquini's 'Sonata in D Minor'. He had once heard that played in the Opera House in Paris, and it had always stuck in his mind. He'd never before been able to whistle it properly, although he'd often tried. Now he was surprised to find the notes being produced quite well . . .

When he stopped whistling, the tumult in his mind had died away. His thoughts were clear again.

'That is one way of making sure that I do not send in a report, *mon commandant*.'

Major Dux attempted to simulate indignation. But the words rang false.

'You are insulting me, Capitaine Monclaire. I've decided to send you because of your obvious knowledge of the Bormones. You need not go alone. You may take any other officer you wish with you.

'I shall go alone, *mon commandant*. There is no reason why two of us should die.'

Major Dux changed his line of pretence, but it was no more convincing than the first.

'You'll not die. Believe me, I'd not send you out there if I thought so. I'm quite convinced that you'll be able to provide me with valuable information as to what it is that the Bormones want . . . and if you would rather go alone, then most certainly do. I'm satisfied that you're quite capable of conducting these nego- tiations yourself.'

Monclaire looked steadily at Dux. He said: 'I've heard many excuses for murder, and many names for it. But this is the first time I've heard it described as a negotiation, *mon commandant*!'

* * *

Dice eased his position behind the rampart. He was in a half-kneeling posture and his left leg was throbbing from the pressure of the stone platform.

For more than an hour he'd been gazing along the sights of his Lebel at the group of fifty Bormones who were within the orbit of his fire. By now, his eyes were heavy with fatigue. So far, the Bormones had done nothing beyond pitching camp and taking up defence positions. He looked at Glass, who was at the next rampart.

'This is going to be a siege,' he said. 'If they were planning to attack, they would have done it before now.'

Glass nodded and rubbed his empty eye socket. He'd taken out his artificial eye for the sake of comfort. At the moment, only the Arabs could see his face, and he was not particular about how he looked to them.

'I guess that's right,' Glass said. 'I'm only hoping this place's got plenty reserves of water.'

'There'll be enough for a couple of weeks, at least. That's the minimum reserve, and I've been told that new supplies were brought in only yesterday.'

Glass said: 'I'm wondering why the Bormones are doing this. I thought they were mostly concerned with the building of Fort Vateau.'

'This could be one way of hindering things at Vateau. While they are round here, we can't get out. That means we can't get to Vateau to look after the place.'

'I figure we could fight our way through this lot.'

'Maybe we could, but we wouldn't be a lot of use after we'd done it. Certainly we wouldn't be in any condition for a long march, and we'd be lucky if there were half of us left.'

Marleigh was at the other rampart next to Dice. Against orders, he'd half-turned and was looking into the parade square below.

At first, he'd only been watching Monclaire idly. He'd seen the captain descend from the watch-tower with the portly Major Dux. Without actually looking, he'd been aware that Monclaire had gone into the officers' mess, and had emerged again a few minutes later. Now he watched him moving towards the gates.

'What the blazes is Monclaire going to do?' Marleigh asked.

His question was heard by several legionnaires besides Dice and Glass. All of them twisted away from the ramparts. They saw that Major Dux was now standing by the pulley mechanism.

The gates at Fort New were of the sliding type. Mounted on a steel track, they opened by parting in the centre and moving into apertures between the massive walls. The operation was controlled by a pulley which was set slightly away from the gates.

They heard Dux give an order to two men who were gripping the wheel on the pulley handle. '*Ouvert!*'

The handle was turned slowly, the men straining under the enormous weights they were dragging apart. There was a noise like distant thunder as the gates moved on their tracks.

On the ramparts, they looked and listened with abject amazement. It was Dice who said: 'Are we going to invite the Bormones in?'

Marleigh said: 'I don't think so. Look at Monclaire. It seems as if he's going out to meet them.'

They looked at Monclaire. Their eyes fastened onto him as though he held some magnetic attraction. He was walking through the gates.

Dux squealed out another order. The gates were closed.

The legionnaires reversed their positions so that they were again looking over the ramparts. Within a few seconds, Monclaire came into view. He was unarmed. In his right hand he held a small square of white material. The material hung limp in the still air, as though aware of its own uselessness as a symbol of truce.

There was a stir of movement among the Bormones. Their riflemen rose from their prone postures and awaited Monclaire, their weapons levelled.

There was something oddly magnificent in the way Monclaire walked towards them. His steps were unhurried, yet they were not slow. It was as though he were approaching a body of his own men prior to an inspection. It was casually courageous — and totally futile.

Peering over the ramparts, the men of

his company watched him reach the nearest of the Bormones. They saw them gather round the Legion officer. They caught a glimpse of the white material as it was torn from his hand. When next they saw it, it was crumpled on the sand.

Then Monclaire disappeared in the midst of a bubbling mass of robed figures.

After a long while, Dice said: 'I'm wondering whose idea that was?'

In fact, he wasn't wondering. He knew. One man only could be responsible.

Glass confirmed Dice's thoughts. 'It wouldn't be Monclaire's. He knows too much about the Bormones to fall for the idea that he'd have any protection from a truce flag. It must have been that guy they call Dux . . . the murdering slob . . . '

A rumble of talk had spread along the ramparts. It was the low-pitched, incredulous talk of men who were bewildered and sickened.

They could no longer see Monclaire. But they could imagine what was happening to him . . . or about to happen to him.

He would not die quickly. The

Bormones had made a perverted art of killing by the slowest of degrees. Of outraging the flesh of men until even the bravest felt his spirit break and he whimpered for mercy. Ghastly, satanic things would be done to him before he at last found the inevitable relief.

To talk while behind the ramparts was a gross contravention of orders. It was the same as talking while on a formal parade. But the men of No. 1 Company did not seem to care, and the indifference spread to the other companies. There are times when any discipline — even Legion discipline — can waver and break. This was one of those times. The men in that fort spent all of their times balanced on a fine edge between life and death. Death itself did not move them much. They had seen it in most of its forms often enough, and human beings can become used to anything. But this was different. This was a case of a man being ordered to conduct his own ghastly execution.

It was natural that in No. 1 Company the revulsion was felt most acutely. Monclaire was *their* officer commanding.

Each of the men knew him well. It would be going too far to state that any of them liked him. An efficient Legion officer cannot be regarded with affection. But almost all respected him. They respected him because, blended with his iron discipline, there was a personal courage which equalled that of any of those he commanded, plus an innate sense of fairness.

As Patruski, the Russian, had once put it: 'All officers are swine. Monclaire is a swine. But he is a good swine.'

Most of the men were now ignoring the order to keep the Bormones under rifle cover. Their Lebels were left lying between the ramparts while they talked huskily. One or two corporals attempted to quiet them, but there was no authority in their efforts. They too felt a mutinous revulsion.

The climax came when they noticed Major Dux.

It happened, as such things so often do, spontaneously without any apparent leadership.

Dux was back in the centre of the

parade ground. As viewed from the top of the walls, he looked fat and pompous. He had just finished talking to Sergeant Duparne. Duparne's face had gone a shade of grey under his deep tan. He saluted the officer, and as Dux walked away, the major suddenly slackened his pace so as to light a cigarette.

Maybe it was the match which flickered in front of the tobacco which created the flashpoint. There was something damnably indifferent about it. Something almost contemptuous. He'd just sent a man to his death, and he chose to enjoy a smoke immediately afterwards, in front of the garrison . . .

There was a burst of whistling — of catcall whistling. The type of sound which is an international language of abuse. It began among No. 1 Company, and inside seconds it had spread along the entire walls. And every face which was producing the sound was turned towards Major Dux.

Dux stopped, half-turned, and looked up. The match fell from his fingers and flickered out on the ground. His cigarette hung unlighted between fat and slack lips.

He did not look up at the legionnaires for long. The great square of hostile faces seemed to crush him. He dropped his head and looked towards Duparne. The sergeant, too, had halted in his stride. Dux tried to swallow away a swelling in his throat, but his voice held a tremble.

'*Sergent!* What is this? Quieten them at once. *Mon Dieu* . . . is it a rabble that we have here? I'll inflict field punishment — '

The last part of his sentence was drowned as the whistling grew louder. Duparne came close to him. His attitude towards Dux was strictly correct in the sense that it would be difficult to define any fault in it. He stood firmly to attention. His answer was respectful. But there was in his tones an inflection which was not usual when an N.C.O. addresses an officer — even a senior N.C.O.

'I'll have to wait a few minutes, *mon officier*. My voice cannot compete against this noise. When they get tired of being indignant, I'll deal with them and try to find who started the uproar.'

'Indignant? You say they're indignant!

What have they to be indignant about?'

'They have just seen an officer killed. To the men of my own company, that is particularly bad, for we thought well of Captain Monclaire.'

Duparne still spoke correctly. But Dux detected the unspoken meaning in the sentence. He looked with some astonishment at Duparne. He'd heard that this N.C.O. had at one time possessed a terrible reputation among the legionnaires. Tales were told of brutality towards men which had shocked even the Legion. True, he was supposed to have become more reasonable of late, but Dux did not know the sergeant had reduced himself to the level of siding with the men.

Dux said: 'Captain Monclaire was doing his duty. If the Bormones kill him, they will be doing no more to him than they have to many others in the Legion.'

'Captain Monclaire was unarmed. He did not have the soldier's privilege of defending his life, *mon officier.*'

Dux did not answer. He turned his back on Duparne and strutted fast towards the officers' mess.

The whistling stopped as Dux disappeared.

When Sergeant Duparne reached the ramparts, the legionnaires regarded him in intense silence. Some went back to their firing positions. Others remained as they were. There was no expression on Duparne's face as he walked along the platform. It was like a dark plaster cast.

It was when he reached a place in the middle of No. 1 Company that he spoke. And his words were strangely quiet. None of them had ever heard Duparne speak thus before.

He said, 'That is not the way, *mes soldats*. Remember, the Bormones still surround us, and many of your ramparts are unguarded. It must be your duty first — and in good time, Capitaine Monclaire will be avenged . . . '

Slowly, he turned back and descended the stone steps. And the legionnaires returned to their ramparts.

6

Dice

When darkness began to creep over the desert and cast shadows within the square of the fort, most of the legionnaires were relieved from the ramparts. There was little danger from the Bormones at night.

Tension on the nerves can exhaust a man as quickly as any purely physical effort. And the effects can be far more complete, for recovery takes longer. Thus it was that the men did not speak much when they returned to their barrack rooms. They flopped onto their bunks and lay very still.

Dice had his eyes closed, but he was not sleeping. On the contrary, his fast-moving, analytical brain was working at top pressure.

Ever since they had set out from Sadazi, Dice had shared the general feeling of approaching crisis. A feeling that in the next few days the scales of Providence would finally tilt one way or another to decide the outcome of the long war between France and the Bormone rebels.

And it would decide more than that.

This had also been a struggle between two men. A struggle between El Dowla, whose name aroused fear in every sandy acre of Morocco, and a little-known American legionnaire. A legionnaire who had enlisted with vengeance as his reason — vengeance which had yet to be satisfied. A legionnaire called Dice Regan.

Dice held no particular affection for the government of France. He'd no reason to like the Legion — few men in it had. But, as he lay in his bunk, he realised anew that if El Dowla was not somehow destroyed, the bitter, sweat-filled years under the Tricolour would be wasted. And he would have failed. Dice disliked failure as much as any man.

He weighed the situation.

If El Dowla prevented the building of the fort at Vateau, he would achieve a major victory. And for France, it would be a first-class military disaster. The Legion would lose face with the ordinary Arab populations, and El Dowla's own status would rise in proportion. A complete Legion withdrawal from Bormone territory would then be likely.

The Bormones would certainly prevent the fort being built if No. 1 Company could not get there to protect the already-terrorised Arab labour. And the company certainly would not get there while this ring of Bormones remained thrown round them.

How to break through . . . how to get out? That was the problem.

Eyes still closed, Dice lighted a cigarette that Marleigh had given to him. He puffed at it fast, jerkily, as though keeping physical pace with the whirring of his mind.

Supposing the ordinary Arabs — the Arabs in the villages — could be persuaded to help? Some of them had already seen the fanatical cruelty of the Bormone warriors, and by now nearly all must have heard of it. They must realise the tyranny that would result if El Dowla gained control and the Tricolour were banished from this area of North Africa. If he could reach just one Arab leader — just one man of courage and intelligence who would lead his people against the Bormones who surrounded them there at Fort Ney . . .

There was such a man!

The realisation came to Dice with the bright suddenness of a thunderbolt. He'd seen the man he wanted to reach only the previous day.

It was Bel Hassal of the village of Balati. The village the Legion had saved.

Dice inhaled the cigarette smoke deeply, then opened his eyes. Marleigh, who was blowing sand out of his Lebel's sights, turned to look at him.

'You've had a long kip,' he said. 'Been dreaming of home?'

'Sure thing,' Dice told him. 'I've been dreaming — but it hasn't exactly been of home.'

He stood up and looked out of the slit windows. Across the shadowed parade square he saw the massive hulk of the walls. He'd made his decision. Maybe it was suicide he was planning, but it would still be worthwhile. Everything in life which was worth more than a dime could only be gained by facing some element of risk. And if he failed to obey his gambling instinct now, he'd never be able to live with himself in the future — if he lived. Yes, his mind was made up, and the first obstacle to be overcome was that wall.

★　★　★

It was around one in the morning.

There was stillness everywhere. All along the great circle of Bormones there was an utter lack of movement as the warriors slept in their tents or dozed behind the butts of their long rifles. On the ramparts, too, there was stillness. The sentries stood as though immovable, gazing with semi-seeing eyes at the silhouettes of the enemy. Below them, the parade square was deserted, and so quiet it seemed as if no person had ever disturbed its shadowy peace. And in No. 1 Company's barrack room, the only sound was the occasional incoherent mumble of a sleeping man.

No one there heard the new and faint sound in the room. A cautious, hesitant suggestion of slow movement as Dice got out of his bunk and pulled on his trousers and tunic. None saw him sling his Lebel across his shoulders and walk on the toes of his boots towards the door. There was only the slightest creaking of hinges as the door opened and closed behind him.

As he stood in the stone corridor, Dice felt a sudden and wild urge to go back. To go back to his bunk, to take off his uniform, and to sleep again . . . before it was too late. There was still time. In another few minutes there would be no retreat. He would be irrevocably committed to a mad, wild course which could lead . . . could lead to anything.

The urge passed. He moved along the corridor, which was lit by a single flickering oil lamp. At the far end a door led onto the company's guard room. This was slightly ajar, and from within there came an occasional mumble of voices and the clatter of iron mugs as the junior N.C.O. and the men in there talked over coffee. Pressed against the opposite wall, Dice edged past the door. Beyond, there was another door. This was open, and it gave out on to the pool of blackness which was the parade square. He felt safer when he got out under the cover of the dark.

From where he stood, the walls could be only dimly seen, for what little moonlight there was had disappeared behind a patch of cloud. But he knew Fort Ney well, and he knew also just where the steps to the ramparts were situated and where the sentries were most likely to be standing. His breath was coming in short and shallow gasps as he crossed the open ground.

The steps were about five feet wide and they were set against the side of the wall. He reached them without trouble, but after mounting the first three he had to pause. In spite of his efforts to tread lightly, his boots were making too much noise on the stone. They would have to be removed.

As he was busy with the operation, he heard a movement above him and some distance to his left. It was the unmistakable sound of a sentry grounding the butt of his rifle. It gave Dice a useful clue as to his exact proximity.

After fastening the boots to his shoulder straps, he ascended the steps in bare feet. This time he moved in absolute silence.

When he reached the level of the rampart platform, he did not stand up. Even in the darkness he might be seen against the background of the sky. Instead, he lay for a few moments on his stomach, listening.

Again he heard a move from the sentry — this time as the man re-slung his Lebel and eased his position slightly. At a rough guess, it seemed to Dice that he was thirty feet away. Maybe a little more.

In his mind, Dice could picture the fellow. Right now he'd be looking towards the desert he could scarcely see, and trying to calculate how long it was before the guard was due to be changed. Dice could have answered that question for him. He had more than half an hour to wait.

It is never easy to reach a dangerous decision when you have plenty of time in which to do so. That was the way Dice found it. He kept putting off the moment when he'd make a dive for the rampart right above him and then risk the thirty-foot drop down the far side. Several times he said to himself, 'Come on — let's go — ' but his body remained inactive. It was as if his flesh rebelled at the risk and refused to obey his brain. But the moment came when mind and muscle worked together. It seemed to happen spontaneously. Dice had no recollection of making a new decision. There was a second when he was still flat below the rampart. Then there was another second when he was upright and the same rampart was between his legs as he sat astride it. Dice gripped the top edge of the gritty stonework with his fingers as he swung over the side. Before he let go, he paused to listen. There was still no sound. He'd been lucky. The sentries had not seen him.

The swing in space immediately before the drop was not pleasant. A physically fit man who knows how can drop thirty feet without hurting himself, providing the landing surface is not too hard. But Dice was acutely aware of two factors which did not make his prospects too bright. First, there were a large number of stones mixed with the sand immediately below. Second, he had a rifle and equipment slung from his shoulders, which added to his weight and could cause serious injury on landing. It would be a final ignominy if he broke a leg outside the fort and was either brought in by the garrison or captured first by the vigilant Bormones.

Relaxing all his limbs, Dice released his grasp from the wall.

The relaxation was important — it is the secret of falling without injury. It is taut muscles which make the bones break under sudden impact. A bare bone can be dropped from a great height without being harmed. But wrap that same bone tightly in paper and drop it — then it will certainly smash in several places. So it was that Dice went down with his limbs hanging loose.

The fall seemed to take a long, long

time, although in fact it was rather under a second. His first awareness that he'd met the ground was after he rolled over twice and he felt a deep, jabbing pain as the butt of his Lebel dug into his ribs. In all, he rolled over five times, but he made no attempts to check the motion. He knew that he'd landed on his heels and buttocks. The impact had thrown him sideways onto his back, and the roll was absorbing the force of the drop.

When he came to rest, he raised himself very slowly. There was no certainty yet that he had not suffered some serious hurt. First, he looked at his arms, then moved them. Several of the fingers were grazed and bleeding, but otherwise they were all right. Next, his legs. There was a tenderness under each of the kneecaps which forewarned of swelling, but nothing seemed to be broken.

Dice sighed. He whispered to himself: 'Buddy, you've got away with that part of it.'

Moving on his hands and knees, despite the pain, he eased away from the fort.

When the walls were forty yards off, he got to his feet and laced on his boots. It was then that he discovered his toes were lacerated, although not seriously.

Dice tried to recollect the exact dispositions of the Bormones.

Although the tents entirely surrounded Fort Ney, their guard posts of riflemen were spread out at intervals of between one hundred and two hundred yards. It was possible, he hoped, to slip between these. Since the rest of the camp was sleeping, there ought not to be a lot of difficulty in getting through it and into the desert beyond.

In relation to his present position, he calculated that he was dead between two groups of guards. If he could hold on to his bearing, and if the moon stayed behind that cloud, he'd only to walk right ahead . . .

A few stars were out, and he fixed his position with one of them before starting. He counted his paces so as to have a guide to the amount of ground he had covered, for the Bormone camp was completely invisible. It was a slow, agonising process. He held his Lebel in his hands. He'd already resolved that if he were seen, he'd use it on himself. That would be better than the fate which had been Monclaire's.

The darkness no longer seemed to be friendly. It no longer appeared to be a shield. Rather, it was a place of silence and mystery out of which there might at any moment come a shout, and a grasping hand, and the awful flash of a curved knife . . .

There were droplets of sweat on his face, and they were not caused by the sultry warmth of the night.

When he had completed six hundred paces, Dice stopped. By now he ought to be level with the guard posts. Still there was no sound, except for the distant neighing of a tethered horse. He instinctively looked in the direction of the animal. For the first time, he saw the outline of the camp. He was able to discern the shadowy silhouettes of the tents. They looked as if they were a couple of hundred yards ahead. But Dice knew that distances are deceptive in the desert. They appear to be less than they actually are because of the absence of intermediary landmarks. Anyway, it was reasonably certain that he was almost through the point of most danger — the point where the armed Bormones were crouched.

He continued yet more slowly. His nerves rasped at each small sound made by his boots on the sand, and his raw fingers were greasy as they grasped the Lebel.

Still the moon stayed behind the cloud patch.

It was when he stumbled against a guy-rope of a tent that Dice knew he had reached the main encampment. He'd been concentrating so acutely upon the possible danger from either side and behind that he'd not seen what lay before him.

If he'd been walking at a normal pace, he'd certainly have been thrown to the ground, for the rope caught him just above the ankles. As it was, he was only temporarily thrown off-balance. But the experience was unnerving. Dice paused again, this time to wipe his brow on the sleeve of his tunic and to regather his wits.

He looked at the tent. It was large for a Bormone military unit to carry. He guessed it must belong to some senior officer. The others grouped around it were much smaller.

It was when he was about to move on that Dice saw something which caused him to alter his mind. It was the figure of a sleeping Bormone warrior. The warrior was sitting outside the tent entrance with a drawn scimitar between his legs.

That he should not have been asleep was beyond doubt, for he was obviously posted there as a guard.

But a guard on whom?

If a Bormone officer were in that tent, it was not likely that the guard would allow himself to fall asleep. That guard must be confident that his services would not be needed during the night.

Dice's eyes travelled back to the tent entrance.

That entrance was not partly open, as was usual. It was laced tight shut with leather thongs.

Dice drew in a hissing breath.

The chances were that a prisoner was in there. A prisoner, perhaps, who was bound so securely that the placing of a guard over him was no more than a formality.

Could the prisoner be Captain Monclaire?

Everyone in Fort Ney had assumed that Monclaire must have been subjected to torture within a few minutes of being captured. But Dice suddenly realised that this need not be so. It was possible, even probable, that he would be kept unharmed until precise orders were received from El Dowla as to what was to be done with him. A captain of the Legion was an exceptional prisoner, and it might well be that the Bormones thought he could give them information before dying.

As he considered the possibilities, Dice came to one of his lightning decisions. He was going to look inside that tent. He knew he'd just have to do that. To pass through the camp without doing so was unthinkable.

He looked quickly around him. The faintest of desert breezes had sprung up, and there was a gentle, almost timid, flapping from the tents. That tethered horse was still neighing. But they were the only sounds. And Dice welcomed them. They gave a touch of substance and realism to an atmosphere which would otherwise be intolerably intense.

He took a couple of long and silent steps towards the sleeping sentry.

The Bormone's turbaned head was slumped forward so that it almost touched the blade of his scimitar. Dice reversed the position of his rifle so that the barrel was gripped between his hands and the butt was held high.

He judged the force of the blow carefully. He wanted it to be hard enough to put the man out of action for an hour at least. But he did not want it to be too hard.

There were two reasons for this caution. Firstly, he did not want to kill the Bormone. Dice was like most western soldiers in that he would kill when he had to, and do it without much regret. But he had a marked repugnance against taking the life of a man who was not in a position to defend himself.

The second reason was more practical.

The human skull is surprisingly hard. So is the butt of a Lebel rifle. A very vigorous blow might be heard despite the turban covering.

The weapon descended in a half-circle. The point of impact was at the temple. It had the speed of a firm downward chop. The Bormone gave out a tiny, childlike gasp. His body rolled forward, then sideways. Dice pulled him into a sitting position again and, with some difficulty, placed him so that to a casual observer he looked much as he had before he passed from a light sleep into deep insensibility.

Next he got to work on the sheepskin lashings which secured the tent entrance. It would have been quicker to have cut these with his knife, but Dice untied the main knot. He wanted to be able to refasten it neatly. When the thongs were loose enough, he put his head into the tent. It was like looking into a full inkwell. There was nothing to be seen save absolute blackness.

Earlier that day, Marleigh had given him a few matches and a cigarette. Both were at a premium in the desert. Dice got out one of the matches and struck it against the sole of his boot. It flickered up, but before he could grasp any detail, the flame was extinguished by the breeze entering the aperture. He said, 'Hell . . . ' and struck another.

This time the flame went up high and straight. Dice blinked round the tent. At first he could not discern much. Just a few skin blankets and the remains of a meal on the sand. Then he saw something in the centre of the tent. Something which made him whisper loudly, 'My God, so he's here — '

Monclaire was there. He was full-length on the ground, and his hands and feet were bound. His tunic was torn open at the front and his black hair was caked with rust. A streak of congealed blood ran down one of his cheeks.

But he was conscious. His eyes were open and he was looking straight at Dice.

Dice pushed himself completely into the tent. As the remains of the match burned his fingers, then died out, he reached Monclaire.

Slowly and precisely, Dice whispered to

him: 'Are you badly hurt?'

There was only a slight pause, then out of the blackness Monclaire breathed an answer.

'*Non, mon legionnaire.* I've been what you Americans call 'beaten up a little', but they are saving the worst for later.'

'They *were* saving it,' Dice corrected. 'I'm aiming to get you out of here. There's no time for me to do any explaining just yet. It may sound kind of silly, but this is a time when a legionnaire gives orders to his captain.'

As he spoke, Dice was opening his clasp-knife.

There was no need now to use more matches. By using his sense of touch he was able to find the bonds. Within a minute he had cut through them.

With the curious courtesy which seldom leaves the French, Monclaire said: '*Merci.* But I'm sorry. My legs are numb. I must wait a while before I can walk.'

Dice had temporarily forgotten the deadening effect of the tight cords round Monclaire's limbs. Quickly, he slackened the officer's leather ankle gaiters and massaged his legs. At first Monclaire could not help, for his arms would scarcely move. But as the blood in them began to flow again, he rubbed at the muscles below his knees. It was all of five minutes before he could stand.

He was leaning slightly on Dice as they moved towards the open tent flap.

They passed slowly through the line of tents. When the moon finally broke through the patch of cloud and showed the Bormone camp clearly, they were well away from it — out in the desert.

7

Bel Hassal

Monclaire had not minimised his sufferings. When he had said he had been 'beaten up a little', he had spoken the exact truth. Upon his seizure by the Bormones, he had been jostled, punched, and threatened with knives. But that was all. Immediately the Bormone officers recognised his status, they decided to preserve the prisoner pending orders from El Dowla.

He revealed this to Dice as they tramped in a northerly direction. It was when they were a full three miles from the camp that Monclaire stopped. He stroked the stubble on his lean chin.

'I did not ask why it was that we did not try to get straight back to the fort,' he said. 'You asked me not to ask questions, and I respected that. But now I must know how you plan to return.'

He spoke crisply. The note of authority

which had been absent since his rescue had now crept back.

Dice said: 'I am not going back to Fort Ney, *mon capitaine*. In any case, I do not think we could do so. The luck I had in getting through the Bormone lines once is not likely to last a second time.'

In the faint moonlight, Dice saw Monclaire stiffen.

'Not going back! Is it that you're mad, Legionnaire? We cannot walk about in the desert. We must at least make the attempt.'

Subconsciously, because of his training, Dice had assumed the position of attention. He became suddenly aware that it was ridiculous in their present plight.

Relaxing, he said: 'I must ask that while we are alone together we forget that you are an officer and I a legionnaire. If we do not, it will be impossible for me to give you an explanation.'

There was a long pause. Monclaire was battling with a lifetime of military tradition. In the end, he nodded.

'As you please. But you must remember that it is I who command.'

The last statement caused Dice to experience a temporary rush of annoyance. But it passed. He realised that Monclaire could scarcely say anything else.

'*Mon capitaine* . . . I did not leave the fort deliberately to rescue you. It was pure accident that I found you, although I'm mighty glad of that accident.'

Monclaire looked shocked. Then he laughed.

'I am glad, too. I have no appetite for being a plaything of El Dowla's. But go on — '

Leaning on the barrel of his Lebel, Dice told him quietly of his plan to contact Bel Hassal. Monclaire listened attentively. Halfway through, he pulled out a cigarette case which had escaped the attention of the Bormones, and he offered it to Dice. He was exhaling a long spiral of smoke down his thin nostrils when Dice finished.

'This isn't any attempt at heroics,' Dice concluded. 'It's our only chance. It's by mobilising the ordinary peaceful Arabs that we might be able to break the siege on the fort. Otherwise — well, I guess the garrison could remain locked in there for months.'

Monclaire shook his head.

'Not for months. The water would not last for more than three weeks — '

He looked at the glowing tip of tobacco and again was silent. Monclaire was an officer with an agile imagination. A man of ideas. That had sometimes proved to be a disadvantage in his military career, for it is unfortunately true that no army can afford to encourage such men. The essence of discipline is routine. Too many new ideas are apt to disturb routine — and discipline at the same time. He found himself frankly intrigued with the plan of this tough, wiry-looking American.

This Legionnaire Regan had served under him for some time now. They had shared many experiences together. He respected the American, and he knew, as men always do, that the respect was reciprocated. But he'd never properly known him. The gulf between their ranks had, up to now, made that impossible. He felt glad that for the time being he'd agreed to bridge that gulf.

Monclaire said: 'I do not think you are doing this just to save your own life, or those of the garrison. And you cannot be so very attached to the Legion. I feel that by the way you talk, and by the things you have done in the past, that you have some deeper reason. It would make things easier if you told me . . . we're alone here, and no one else will know . . . '

His voice had changed. There was nothing sentimental about it, nothing false. But it held the overtones of man who was wanting to understand another man. Dice detected them.

He said: 'I had a brother. He was a good guy. He was murdered by the Bormones.'

'I'm sorry. Will you believe me when I say I'd always thought it was something like that? You are . . . you are different, *mon ami*, from the usual type of legionnaire. Yet you never seemed to me to be the sort who'd enlist to escape some personal trouble. There are others like you too. Some are in my company and are your friends, I believe — I think some strange stories could be told of why men join this international army of France.'

Dice said, 'I've a personal interest in the Bormones. If they are not destroyed — then all my time in this uniform will have been wasted. And most of all, I guess I want to see El Dowla finished.'

'Then I think that what you propose is our only chance. I suppose I ought to say that you have been foolish — that technically you are a deserter; and not for the first time, *mon ami*. But I agree with you. We'll try to reach Balati; and there, if fortune is with us, we'll talk with Bel Hassal.'

Simultaneously they dropped their cigarettes in the sand and again set their steps to the north.

Balati was slightly more than twenty miles from Fort Ney. That is not a great distance to cover on foot if you are moving on a smooth surface. But when your boots are sinking deep into rocky sand; when you are weary before you start; when, with less than a quarter of the distance covered, the grilling Sahara sun comes up and you've only a three-pint water bottle between two of you . . . then it is not easy. In fact, it is the concentrated essence of hell.

And, at the back of their minds, Dice and Monclaire had always the possibility of being found by the Bormones.

It was certain that the Bormones would search for Monclaire. But they counted on them assuming that he would attempt to get back to the fort, so the area of the search was not likely to be extensive.

Monclaire had a wristwatch. At the end of every hour they rested for five minutes. Every two hours they each took a sip of water. But by mid-day, they were both in a weak condition.

When their five-minute rest period was over, they found it a struggle to get to their feet. Their entire bodies were enveloped in sweat, as though they had been submerged in a bath of grease. Sand was in their hair, in their eyes and nostrils, even in their mouths. Their throats were tender and swelling through want of water.

Dice croaked slightly as he spoke.

'I guess we've still got at least six miles to cover — I'm kind of wondering whether we'll be able to do it.'

Monclaire did not answer. He was watching the eastern horizon. Dice's eyes followed in that direction. A long smudge could just been seen, and it appeared to be approaching very slowly.

'It could be the Bormones,' Monclaire said.

'I don't think so,' Dice answered. 'They're not moving fast enough for Bormone cavalry.'

It was half an hour later that they knew for certain. It was an Arab caravan. For a few seconds the realisation made them laugh in a wild, stupid sort of way. They stumbled forward to meet it.

The caravan consisted of six camels and double that number of Arabs. They looked with astonishment at the two desperate men in Legion uniform, and one or two fumbled nervously with their muskets.

Monclaire spoke to them in fluent Arabic. Yes, it seemed they were going to Balati to trade some silks. They would carry the legionnaires on their camels thus far, but they'd want payment . . .

Monclaire assured them that they'd receive payment, and they were helped onto the animals. As they travelled, they were given water and they ate goat meat.

It was mid-afternoon when they re-entered Balati. They immediately dismounted the camels, and Monclaire noted particulars of the leader of the caravan so that payment could be arranged — if they lived to make such arrangements.

They were fresher and stronger now. They walked almost briskly through the narrow, fetid streets. At first, they were watched curiously by the population. Then they were followed by a chattering, excited mob. Arab children ran and skipped around their legs.

Monclaire smiled as he glanced at Dice.

'We are causing a sensation,' he said. 'But it is natural. They did not expect to see us again so soon — and looking as we do.'

They reached the market square. A dozen or more stalls were out, and the traders were shrieking and gesticulating of the merits of their wares. But they gradually became silent as Dice and Monclaire moved into their midst.

Monclaire selected a trader and went up to him. 'We wish to find Bel Hassal. Where is his dwelling?'

Deliberately, Monclaire had put the question in an undertone. But the precaution was useless. A surge of eager voices rang out. Above all else, the Arabs like to show people the way. Dozens of them were now simultaneously trying to tell him how to find Bel Hassal. The mass of information was quite incomprehensible. But in the end the trader managed to shout a few instructions in Monclaire's ear, and they moved off again, the mob still behind them.

Like all the others, Bel Hassal lived in a mud hovel. It was, however, larger than most, and the alley in which it was situated was comparatively clean. He was squatting outside it and his palm stick was between his bare and scraggy knees. His beard shook with astonishment as he saw Monclaire and Dice, then he got unsteadily to his feet. As he spoke, there was an anxious look on his crinkled face, but he left no doubt as to their welcome.

'We are honoured to see you again so soon — but you look as though the vultures have had you — '

'Bel Hassal, the vultures very nearly did have us,' Monclaire answered. 'We have come to you for help, for we believe that after what you saw yesterday you must be a friend of France.'

The people were pressing round them, listening avidly. Bel Hassal seemed to be about to make some reply when he became aware of them. He shook his stick at them and the mob eased reluctantly away. There was no denying the influence he possessed in the village. Then he indicated the low entrance to his hovel.

'It is all I have to offer,' he said simply. 'But we can speak there in quiet.' He bent almost double and led the way into the hot semi-darkness.

They sat on goatskin rugs while Bel Hassal poured thick black coffee into tiny cups. It was after they had drunk this that Monclaire gestured towards Dice.

'This legionnaire is best fitted to tell of what happened and what we need. He has my permission to speak freely.'

It was a surprise to Dice. In the last few hours, he had naturally left the leadership to Monclaire. But his command of Arabic was good. He outlined the situation in a few clear phrases. When he had done, Bel Hassal gestured for their cups and silently refilled them. When that was finished, he spoke.

'After what happened at Karak, and after what so nearly happened here in Balati, I do indeed know of the scourge El Dowla would be upon our land. I am your servant to do what I can to help those in Fort Ney. But what can I do? I think you speak too generously of my powers when you say that I could rally the others. But even supposing that I did that — what then? In the villages we are but ill-armed people. Ours are not the arts of war, and many of our youngest and strongest are at Vateau building that fort.'

His words, quietly spoken, were so logical that Dice felt a wave of sick depression. But he overcame it and gripped Bel Hassal's wrist as he spoke.

'We believe your influence is great. You are respected here in Balati, and you must also be respected in the other villages round here. We do not need many of your men to break the ring round Fort Ney. Find me just two hundred who can shoot and have courage, and the work can be done.'

Monclaire glanced up at him. The number mentioned seemed ridiculously small. He wondered what this incredible American had in mind, but he did not ask.

Bel Hassal stroked his greasy strands of beard. Then he flicked a cluster of flies away from round his eyes.

'I will get you two hundred men,' he said. 'It is on my oath. At this hour on the morrow, they shall be assembled in Balati.'

8

Bel Hassal's Warriors

They slept that night in Bel Hassal's hovel, though the old Arab was not there. He was still absent when they woke at dawn, but soon after daylight a change began to be noticeable in Balati. The marketplace started to fill with men — men on donkeys, men on shaggy horses, even men on camels. All were armed, after a fashion. Most carried aged and long-barrelled muskets. A few only had swords or long knives. Not many were young. On average, they appeared to be past their physical best. But Dice's eyes glittered as he watched them.

'The old man's done it,' he said. 'They may not look much, but they can do.'

Monclaire opened his cigarette case. There was a single cigarette inside. He broke it and handed one half to Dice.

'They will make an extraordinary army,

mon ami. I have not asked you before, but you must tell me now — how do you imagine that these fellows will defeat a thousand of El Dowla's trained troops? *Ma foi!* They are excellent men, no doubt, but we are soldiers and we know other soldiers. Can you say you recognise any here?'

Dice drew deeply on the tobacco. Monclaire was obviously disturbed. He decided that this was the time to reveal what was in his mind. He began by putting a question.

'Is it not a military axiom that the power of surprise is greater than the power of numbers?'

'*Mais oui*. That is elementary. Every junior officer knows that. But you must have the means to create a surprise, and to exploit it. I do not see how it can be done with these ill-armed and undisciplined Arabs. In battle, it is necessary to know that when you give an order it will be carried out in exactly the way you wish. Have you that much confidence in these men of Bel Hassal's? They may mean well; but they would not obey you, my friend, or me.'

'They would obey Bel Hassal. I want him to take command. I will tell him what to do, and I've a hunch that the old man will see that it is done. He's no fool, and I daresay he knows the desert as well as any man breathing.'

Monclaire looked thoughtful.

'It is possible . . . but what is it that you expect them to do? You have not yet told me how they can relieve the fort.'

'By using the cover of darkness. Obviously there can be no question of a direct attack. But those Arabs can approach the fort quietly and unseen. They can group themselves in formations of about twenty each, so that all of the Bormone camp is within musket range. At a signal they can open fire together. They may not hit very much, but I'll wager they'll cause panic among the Bormones, for they won't know the strength of the enemy. And it's a certainty that the fort garrison will open up too when they hear the shooting. If that doesn't cause the Bormones to withdraw — then they're even tougher than I thought.'

A slow smile creased Monclaire's

brown face. He toyed with his moustache.

'*Oui*, I think it is possible. You Americans are amazing people, *mon legionnaire* . . . '

*   *   *

It was at sunset that Bel Hassal reappeared. He came on a mule at the head of the last detachment of men. These assembled with the others in the market.

They presented a fantastic spectacle. Even Dice's optimism was slightly dimmed as he surveyed them. It was as though some weird burlesque was being given in Balati.

The air vibrated under the braying and grunting of the animals, under the chatter of their owners, under the excited conjectures of the watching population. There was no semblance of order. All were packed together in a conglomeration of men and beasts.

Bel Hassal salaamed to Dice and Monclaire. Dice noticed that the old man must have reserves of strength, for although he must have travelled far during the day and spoken much, he did not look much weaker than usual.

'I have upheld my oath. Here are your men, and they will do your bidding, for they hold a great hate and fear of El Dowla.'

Dice gripped his hand.

'You have done magnificently, but still more is wanted of you. I want you to take charge of these men. I want you to start leading them now to Fort Ney so that you'll reach it before daylight tomorrow.'

He half-expected him to protest. But Bel Hassal did not. It even seemed that there was a slight straightening of his bent figure. As if within him there had been lighted some dim spark of martial desire.

Twice, in the minutest detail, Dice explained to him what he wanted. When Bel Hassal repeated the orders clearly and intelligently, Dice knew that he could be relied upon.

Then, without a lot of confidence, he said: 'Can you get the men formed into three lines? I want to talk to them.'

Bel Hassal briefly inclined his head and turned away from them. He hobbled slowly to the centre of the square and raised his hands. The talking died away and only the sounds from the animals remained. Bel Hassal gave the order and the Arabs began to form themselves into the files. It was a slow, laborious business, particularly as they insisted on dragging their beasts with them. But at last they achieved the simple formation.

Dice ran his eyes carefully along the ranks. He felt reassured. True, these were no soldiers. They were ordinary men — Arabs, as it happened, but much the same as ordinary people all over the world. And they had something which made the common man unconquerable. They had a fierce hatred of tyranny and injustice. Instinctively, Dice knew that while none of them wanted to die, they were not afraid to do so.

Dice told them that they would be under the orders of Bel Hassal. In the barest terms, he told of the situation at Fort Ney, and of the threat to them all from El Dowla. He outlined his plan.

Monclaire followed. Like many of his race, the Frenchman was a natural orator.

France, he said, would not forget those who had served them in this hour of crisis.

When he had finished, there was a shuffle in the lines as the Arabs eased their positions. A pair of old and emaciated horses were produced for Dice and Monclaire. Bel Hassal was helped onto a fresh donkey. With the three at their head, the warriors of Bel Hassal moved off.

Dice estimated that the twenty miles would be covered in about six hours. This was based on the speed of the slowest donkeys — and some of them were very slow. It also allowed a total of one hour for rest periods. With luck, they ought to be taking up their positions near the Bormones at about two o'clock in the morning.

But it didn't work out that way. The delaying incident occurred within an hour of starting. The Arabs had formed themselves into groups, each group comprising the inhabitants of a village. Thus, each rode among friends. This appeared to have distinct advantages, until . . .

A donkey stumbled, throwing its owner

on to the sand. He was middle-aged, and rather fat. As his friends gathered round, he lay flat on his stomach, groaning. Dice made a quick examination of him. As a result, he was sure that the only injury was a slightly wrenched ankle.

'You'd better return to Balati,' Dice said.

He was astonished at the reception accorded his suggestion. The other Arabs broke into an excited chorus of protest. Certainly they would not let the fellow return to Balati on his own. He was their friend, therefore they would all go back with him and catch up with the main body later. He might be badly hurt. He might be waylaid and unable to defend himself. No — they would all escort him to Balati.

Dice groaned, and glanced desperately at Monclaire. The captain looked as unhappy as the legionnaire.

It was some time before Dice could make himself heard. Then he said: 'Your friend is but slightly hurt, and we're only a few miles from Balati. He'll be quite safe by himself.'

The protest chorus sounded anew.

They were not convinced. The foot was painful, was it not? It might well be broken. They could not abandon their friend. When they had conducted him to safety, they would quickly be back.

That was just what Dice doubted. The double journey would be a big additional strain on their already none-too-fresh mounts. If they were allowed to do as they wished, they might well find themselves left hopelessly behind.

Dice made a decision. About twenty men were involved, and that number would not make a vital difference to their fighting strength. Therefore the only course was to give way to this manifestation of traditional Arab loyalty.

'Perhaps you speak wisely,' he said. 'Conduct him to Balati, and there take good care of him. If you find that you cannot overtake us before dawn, do not worry. There are enough of us.'

This time, his words were received with silent disapproval. Nothing was said, but it was obvious that they did not like the prospect of missing battle with the

Bormones. Seeing this, Dice added: 'It will be for you to decide. But I fear you'll not be able to reach us again in time.'

They assured him confidently that they would. Then they set off on the return journey while the remainder of the force pressed towards Fort Ney.

The lost time might have been picked up, but for the fact that the rest periods tended to become longer. Because it was essential that they should arrive fresh, Dice and Monclaire had agreed on a ten-minute pause in every hour. But as the night progressed, it became increasingly difficult to prevent these periods doubling in length.

This was not due to any real reluctance on the part of the Arabs. It was simply due to the fact that they were not soldiers and there was little real discipline. It was usually several minutes after Bel Hassal had given the order to remount that they were again in the saddle. Some of them had trouble with the saddles, some argued in groups about nothing in particular. On one maddening occasion a dozen of them decided to dismantle and clean their muskets. All the others were kept waiting while the ancient weapons were hastily reassembled.

Thus it was nearly three o'clock, little more than an hour before dawn, when Dice, who was riding ahead, saw the distant battlements of Fort Ney.

The moon was behind the fort, and it showed up like a grim fantastic toy in a child's shadow game. Vaguely, he could also discern the surrounding circle of the Bormone camp.

This was the critical time — the time when Bel Hassal's men must take up their positions silently and unseen. If they were detected now, the result would be a massacre.

But Dice need not have worried. Bel Hassal halted his little army, and with surprisingly little trouble he divided them into four groups of rather less than fifty men each. When that was done, he rode over to Dice and Monclaire. It was Monclaire who indicated the positions which the groups should take up. Dice was glad to leave that task to him. It fell within the realm of tactics, a subject on which Monclaire was a master — like most French officers. Whatever might go wrong, Dice knew that under Monclaire's guidance the best possible fighting dispositions would be taken.

The second phase was the movement into position. Of necessity, this took time. Each group had to approach to within a couple of hundred yards of the camp, and they had to do it in absolute silence. There was a squad at each point of the compass, so that every section of the Bormone ring would come under fire. For two of the sets, this involved a lengthy detour.

Monclaire took charge of the most distant group. Dice took over the one which had the shortest distance to move. Bel Hassal personally commanded the third, and the last group was under the orders of a man selected by him.

The mounts were left tethered a clear half-mile from the camp.

Before they parted, Dice and Monclaire briefly shook hands. It was an instinctive gesture, but somehow both felt that they wanted to do it.

It was not the first time that Dice had been impressed by the silence and speed with which the average Arab can move across the desert. His own efforts to crawl seemed clumsy when compared with those of the robed figures around him. Despite the fact that they were holding cumbersome muskets, they seemed to glide forward. They reached their position without incident or difficulty.

It had been decided to allow thirty minutes for the others to prepare. Monclaire was to give the signal to open fire. This was to take the form of a single musket shot.

The details of the Bormone tents were clearly visible to Dice as he waited. His nerves felt raw, on edge. He wondered whether the others would get to their places as easily as they had done.

He looked at the Arabs, who were now flat on their stomach on either side of him. He felt reassured. Their weapons were ready to hand, and there was no suggestion of emotion on their dark, lean faces. Dice thought: 'I wish they were all holding Lebels, the same as me, then I'd

130

feel a hell of a lot better. The trouble with those guns is going to come after the first round. Most of them are only single-shooters, some even muzzle-loaders, and they must take a full half-minute to reload . . . '

It was almost impossible to believe that out there in the desert more than a hundred other men were taking up their positions. Nothing could be seen of them.

Dice was about to whisper something to the nearest Arab — a few inconsequential words to ease the tension — when the signal came.

They had all been expecting it, all were strained waiting for it. Yet somehow it had an element of surprise. The slightly hollow, choking explosion sounded weak in the vastness of the night. It was followed by a moment of silence. But only a moment.

Dice pulled his Lebel to his shoulder, pushed free the safety catch, and squeezed the tripper.

His sights were on the nearest tent, a medium-sized one which looked as though it might be sheltering a dozen

Bormones. But he did not know whether his shot hit it. He did not even hear the detonation of his own cartridge. The noise was drowned by a simultaneous crash of musketry around him. And the tent, with several others, suddenly became a mass of shreds. It crumpled slowly and reluctantly to the ground, as though it were a deflated balloon.

As he jerked back the bolt to eject the spent shell, Dice glanced at what could be seen of the circle of the camp. The effect of that first fusillade was greater than he'd dared to hope. Scarcely a tent was left standing. Already Bormones were emerging from under the slashed material, looking like bewildered white ants. Their voices could be heard. Frightened voices. Voices of men in pain. Voices of men trying to give orders.

But the next round was not nearly so effective as the first.

It was ragged, uneven, due to the fact that some of the Arabs reloaded much faster than others. This fusillade was spread out over the better part of a minute.

The essence of effective small-arms fire is concentration. Every weapon must fire at the same moment. Because this did not happen, many of the Bormones were able to throw themselves flat, thus becoming almost invisible targets.

But the panic in the camp was not lessened. Dazed with the dregs of sleep, they did not know who was firing upon them, where exactly their enemy was, or their strength. All they knew was that death was coming out of the darkness.

Dice emptied the eight rounds in his magazine in the time it took the others to fire a couple of shots. As he pressed in a new clip, he looked anxiously at the fort. At that moment, the sight and sound for which he'd been hoping materialised. There was a series of pink flashes from the ramparts. Then the distant whip-like cracks of Lebels. The fort had opened fire.

The men in Fort Ney did not do any material damage to the Bormones, because the range was too long. But they added to the chaos.

The Bormones in the guard positions

returned fire at the fort, but it was a sheer waste of ammunition. Yet they could not do even that for long, for the other panic-stricken men began to run aimlessly across their line of fire.

It became apparent that many of the Bormones were unarmed. They had either forgotten or been unable to retrieve their weapons when the tents collapsed on them.

It was less than five minutes after the firing of Monclaire's signal shot that the Bormones streamed away from the remnants of their camp, away from the fort. And as they ran into the forbidding blackness of the desert, they were followed by a barrage of musketry.

9

The Major's Decision

Major Dux liked life to be orderly. He had a strong preference for the natural sequence of things. For example, he preferred to be awake during the day and to sleep during the night. Even when on active service, he tried to organise his duties so that the could achieve this. Therefore he was distinctly displeased when awakened by the sound of firing somewhere in the vicinity of the fort.

At first, he thought of ignoring the matter and resuming his sleep. It was probably just some minor incident among the Bormones. Then he remembered that the Bormones scarcely ever attacked during the hours of darkness.

Something unusual must be happening. He sat up in bed.

A new sound reached his unwilling ears. It was the much closer and louder sound of shooting from the ramparts. Most certainly something was wrong. He dragged on his trousers and tunic over his silk pyjamas. He swore heavily as he did so.

The door opened and his orderly, a corporal, came in and saluted.

'*Mon officier*, the officer of the guard asks for your presence. Something is happening in the desert.'

Dux pushed past the man. As he crossed the parade square he saw that a general stand-to had already been ordered. Men were streaming out of their barrack rooms and up the steps to the ramparts.

The officer of the guard was a slightly nervous young lieutenant. Dux liked his subordinates to be nervous. It added to his own sense of superiority.

He waved a plump hand towards the camp. 'What is this? What's happening?'

The lieutenant cleared his throat. Then he stammered out some answer which was lost amid the rifle fire. Dux pushed him aside. Then he noticed Sergeant Duparne. Duparne was standing just behind the lieutenant, and there was an odd, calculating expression on his face.

'You, Sergent. Do you know what's going on?'

'No. But I think the Bormones are in trouble, *mon officier*. They are obviously being fired upon. Look . . . their tents are collapsing.'

'Who would fire on them?'

Duparne shrugged his shoulders. There was something faintly, very faintly, insolent about the gesture. But his answer was respectable enough.

'I do not know. But I think we'll have the answer soon.'

A series of shouts broke out from some of the legionnaires. They were the first to see that the Bormones were retreating away from the fort. Indeed, it was more than a retreat. It was intolerable to Dux that this should be happening and he did not know anything about it. It made him feel helpless, impotent.

'Put on the searchlights,' he ordered.

The three mobile lights jumped into vivid life. Their intense beams played over the sand. They showed the fallen tents, the sprawled figures of Bormones who would fight no more. And in the far distance they revealed the fast-disappearing lines of warriors.

Then one of the lights picked out something else. It picked out crowds of other Arabs — Arabs who were not Bormones. They were rising from the ground at points all round the fort and rushing towards each other.

And among them, easily noticeable, was a Legion officer and a legionnaire.

Dux's small round eyes dilated. He had the sensation of living a nightmare. He wanted to say something, say anything, but no words would come. He dragged his gaze to Duparne. The sergeant was stroking his chin. There was exultation in his tones as he spoke to Dux.

'It seems that Capitaine Monclaire has survived, *mon officier*. And the other is surely Legionnaire Regan.'

The words came to Dux. They came in a torrent.

'How can Monclaire have survived? And that legionnaire . . . he is a deserter. There'll be a swift treatment for him.'

'It seems they have organised a relief of this fort, *mon officier*.'

Dux swore. Somehow the fort did not seem important now. Nothing seemed important except the fact that Monclaire was alive, and he was consorting with a deserter. He wondered what his exact powers were over an officer in such cases. He was fairly certain that, under the emergency clauses of the manual of military law, he had the power to order his arrest pending investigation by a general officer. He decided to make certain.

Like most soldiers of his type. Major Dux had an extensive knowledge of army regulations. It was almost his favourite reading matter. His spirits revived at the prospect of turning again to that thick, yellow-backed book . . .

'Tell Capitaine Monclaire that I wish to see him in my room as soon as he enters the fort,' he told the lieutenant.

Major Dux left the ramparts and made his way briskly towards his volume of military law.

★　★　★

Monclaire said: 'You do not look very pleased at my return. Is it that you find the shock too much?'

Major Dux frowned and played with his pencil. He looked with distaste at the dirty, dishevelled officer who was sitting at the other side of his desk. Nor did he like the openly cynical and bantering tones he was using. It seemed that he was having to tolerate a lot of insolence among the garrison lately. Too much insolence.

'Naturally, I'm pleased that you're safe. But I told you that no real risk was attached to your approach to the Bormones.'

'We do not agree on this matter of what constitutes a risk. But I'm not interested in debating that now, Major Dux. I intend on making a full report at the proper time, as I believe I once told you. For the moment, it ought to suffice that I can now take my company on to Vateau. That is largely due to the help of the Arabs — and to the enterprise of Legionnaire Regan, who freed me from the Bormones and was responsible for the entire planning of the relief.'

'Legionnaire Regan is a deserter.'

140

'Technically, yes. But he did not leave the fort with the object of desertion. On the contrary, his aim was to save lives, and in that he has succeeded most admirably.'

Dux got sharply to his feet. He strode towards the window. The dawn had now broken and the sky was already becoming blue.

'Are you making excuses for this man? If so, you're wasting your time. Just before you came in here I gave orders for his arrest. I intend to hold a formal court-martial within the hour, and immediately afterwards he will be executed . . . '

At first Monclaire looked steadily at the pencil which Dux had left on the desk. Then his head turned slowly towards the window.

'You have a very precise sense of justice, Commandant.'

'I cannot take any other course. But that is not all. You have been willingly assisting this deserter when your duty was to arrest him. I'm placing you under open arrest, Capitaine Monclaire.'

Monclaire pressed his lips together.

'You are in a drastic mood. Are you sure you can do that?'

'Perfectly sure. I've just checked the regulations. It come under the clause relating to abject failure in duty.'

A more discerning man than Dux would have noted the brittle edge which had crept into Monclaire's normally soft voice.

'So I'm under arrest, and Legionnaire Regan is to be killed. *Mon Dieu*, you're a brave man when it is a matter of seeing other men die, *mon commandant*.'

Dux spun round.

'This is insolence! Remember, *s'il vous plaît*, I am commandant of this fort.'

When he had entered the room, Monclaire had felt a deep fatigue. That fatigue had gone now.

'You make it impossible for me to forget.'

He too rose from his chair. He crossed to the window and stood within inches of Dux. The two stared hard at each other.

Monclaire added: 'You have tried to murder me, but I did not totally blame you for that. I thought it was a result of your own stupidity more than any direct criminal intent. But I do not intend that one of my legionnaires shall receive the bullets of a firing squad for no reason other than that he has shown courage and enterprise.'

'You have no say in the matter, Capitaine Monclaire. You forget that you yourself are under arrest. I shall ring for the orderly officer to take charge of you. I've changed my mind. Your arrest will no longer be open. You will be confined to the mess.'

Dux crossed back to the table and stretched for the handbell which lay there.

His hand closed round the bell. But he did not ring it. It remained suspended in the air while he considered a new situation — a situation in which the bicep muscles of his right arm were suddenly encased in a strong grip, a grip which made further movement impossibly painful. Monclaire's long and strong fingers seemed to bite into his flesh like hot claws.

'*Capitaine!* Are you mad? Release my arm at once.'

If anything, the pressure increased slightly. Dux dropped the bell onto the desk. It rolled to the floor.

Monclaire was standing directly behind Dux. He looked with distaste at the gross and shapeless neck in front of him. Then his eyes moved down. They moved until they were fixed on the major's pistol holster. He extended his free hand, loosened the press-button flap, and extracted the automatic weapon. Then he stepped back a pace, releasing his hold on Dux's biceps.

The major wheeled round. His small and weak jaw appeared to unhinge as he absorbed the fact that the pistol — his own pistol — was levelled at the point directly between his eyes. A stinging surge of hot juice leapt from his belly to his throat. His brain started to spin. Major Dux was frightened. Very frightened.

'Return my gun, *capitaine!* You must indeed have become mad.'

He looked wildly at Monclaire's face. That face had changed. There was no mercy in it; and no hate, either. It was expressionless and indifferent — like an executioner. When Monclaire spoke there was no emotion in his words. They were like a flat, disinterested pronouncement of judgment.

'Fools are often the worst of criminals, Commandant Dux. That is the best that can be said for you. This pistol is to go off by accident . . . you understand. I would rather I did not have to do this, but when the lives of many hundreds of men are in the balance, I'd be failing in my duty if I did otherwise. You need not fear for your reputation. I shall stress that you were an excellent commandant — and your loss was a severe blow.'

The muscles around Dux's mouth started to tremble. His eyes filled with moisture. He made an effort to speak, but no words would come. All he could see now was the dark interior of the pistol barrel . . .

The cylinder of lead lifted up the top of Dux's head. While he was still on his feet, a small amount of grey material which had been his brain flowed over his cheeks.

He fell on to his back, immediately below the desk. Monclaire put the gun inside the warm but lifeless right hand, and closed the fingers round the butt. He was bending over the remains of the major when Dux's orderly knocked on the door and came in.

Monclaire glanced up at the astonished man.

'Commandant Dux has had an accident while cleaning his pistol,' he said. 'He must have forgotten that it was loaded. I fear it is too late to do anything, but send for the medical officer immediately . . . '

10

Rebellion

The medical officer shook his grey head sadly.

'The commandant was not very clever,' he said. 'But I should have thought he could have handled his own pistol without killing himself. Ah, well — he must have been an even greater fool than we thought.'

Monclaire gave a humourless smile, and they watched the blanket-covered stretcher being carried out. Then he said: 'That sort of accident is not unknown. In fact, it can easily happen.'

The medical officer looked curiously at Monclaire. He appeared to hesitate. In the end, he said:

'You say that Dux was cleaning the gun ... He must have been holding it in a — a very curious position for it to be aimed at the most vulnerable part of his body. We do not usually look straight into the barrel of a pistol under such circumstances, even if we forget the obvious precaution of unloading it.'

Monclaire was going through a period of reaction. He knew that he'd done the only possible thing. But now that it was over, he felt sick as he thought about it. And obviously this doctor suspected. He'd not had time to consider such a detail, but he ought to have done so.

'Then you're not satisfied as to the cause of the commandant's death?'

Their eyes met. Now it was the medical officer who tried to smile.

'I am quite satisfied. The cause was a bullet in the head. That is clear enough. How it was fired is another matter. I may have my own opinion about that, Capitaine Monclaire, but I propose to keep it to myself. I think it is better that the commandant is no longer with us . . . '

He moved quietly out of the room. For a long time Monclaire looked at the door through which he had passed. Deliberately, he was waiting. Waiting for the feeling of unsteady sickness to go. Unconsciously, he'd moved into Dux's chair. It was the realisation of that fact which abruptly cleared his mind.

He was entitled to sit there, for he was now the senior officer in Fort Ney. His were the orders which now must be obeyed. He groped for the handbell, then he remembered. It was still on the floor. He was about to stand up to retrieve it when the door re-opened. Sergeant Duparne stood at attention just inside the threshold.

Monclaire felt ridiculously glad of his presence. Duparne and he had served together for many years. They understood each other. Monclaire told him to come in and stand easy.

'You've heard of the — the accident to Commandant Dux?'

Duparne smiled. It was odd, but it was very like the smile the medical officer had given.

'*Oui, mon capitaine*. It was very unfortunate, but I do not think the men are so very disturbed.'

Duparne added: 'I'm here about

Legionnaire Regan. He's under arrest, and . . . '

'Release him. There is no charge against him.'

Duparne looked pleased. Then he said: 'There is another matter. It is the Arabs who helped you. Their leader, a fellow calling himself Bel Hassal, is waiting outside. He wishes to speak with you.'

Monclaire had temporarily forgotten Bel Hassal. He felt guilty.

'But of course — send him in.'

The physical strain was having its effect on Bel Hassal. His surprising reserves of energy seemed now to be gone. He was leaning heavily on his palm stick as he advanced to the chair which Monclaire held out. But there was a glitter of excitement in his old eyes.

'I bring you news,' he said, breathing heavily between each word. 'It has arrived with the twenty of our brothers who returned to Balati.'

Monclaire's mind flashed back to the little group of men with whom Dice had vainly argued in the desert.

'So they have reached us at last — a

little late, I fear.'

Bel Hassal tugged excitedly at his robes.

'Late to fight, but the message they bring is of more importance than their skill in battle.'

Monclaire told him to carry on. Bel Hassal had an inborn sense of the dramatic. He could not forego the effect of a pause in which his listener waited anxiously.

'The whole desert is in revolt against El Dowla,' he said at last. 'The story of the massacre of Karak has now spread to every village and every town of the Bormone lands, and there is a terrible fury abroad. Everywhere they are taking up arms to challenge the armies of El Dowla. Everywhere they are prepared to die rather than live beneath the tyranny of he and his warriors.'

Monclaire felt his heartbeat quicken. Throughout his long years of service in Morocco he'd hoped that one day something like this would happen. He'd hoped that the ordinary Arabs would see that the Bormone warrior caste were not liberators, but enslavers. Now it had come to pass. The frightened people of Karak had died to some purpose.

If this spirit of rebellion could be harnessed, if it could be directed while it was at white heat, then it might be possible to break forever the power of El Dowla.

With an effort, Monclaire stifled his flights of imagination, and directed his mind to vital details.

'Tell me what your people are hoping to do,' he said. 'It is not enough that they seize arms and threaten the Bormones. What action are they hoping to take?'

Here Bel Hassal extended his arms hopelessly.

'Alas, that is the misfortune. They say they are going to march on El Dowla's headquarters at Haratzo, but I fear for them in such a venture . . . '

Monclaire placed a hand against his temple. It had started to throb. The prospect horrified him. He could see it vividly. The Arabs from hundreds of villages marching in small groups on Haratzo. Without discipline, without any real plan . . . they would be methodically sliced to pieces by the Bormone cavalry. It must not be allowed to happen.

Bel Hassal's croaking voice broke in on the mental tumult.

'Already, many men are moving to Vateau,' he was saying. 'There they hope to join with the young men who are building your Legion fort before setting forth with them to El Dowla's city . . . '

The words had the effect of a physical blow. Monclaire slumped back in the chair. That fort just *had* to be completed, and they were proposing to take away those who were working on it in order that they might be massacred in a hopeless battle with the Bormones!

Something, anything, must be done to stop this.

He looked at Bel Hassal. The old Arab obviously knew that his people were organising themselves into a terrible doom. But did he realise that they were doing precisely what El Dowla would have wished by stopping — probably for good — the building of Fort Vateau?

This was sheer tragedy. At last, the

peaceful people of Morocco were at one with the Legion. Yet with their disorganisation they were threatening the existence of the very army they wished to help . . .

Bel Hassal could be of no further assistance. He had done more than could be expected of one frail old man. The initial excitement had left him now as he sat there opposite Monclaire. Suddenly he looked very unhappy as well as very weary. Monclaire was moved to pity. He rose and put a hand on the tattered robes which covered a scrawny shoulder.

He said gently: 'Bel Hassal, you have been of great service to the Legion and to the government of France. You shall be well rewarded.'

Bel Hassal shook his head slowly.

'I do not wish for reward, for what can I have that could be of any use to such an old man? I hope only that you may yet save my people from their own foolishness.'

Monclaire spoke to him again. He told him that he must stay at the fort until he felt stronger. Anything he needed would be put at his service.

As Bel Hassal trudged out of the room, Monclaire's mind was already grappling anew with the problem. He glanced at the big wall map. Vateau was little more than a day's march. There was a possible solution . . .

He sent again for Sergeant Duparne.

Monclaire repeated to him Bel Hassal's report. When he'd finished, Duparne said: 'I already knew most of it, *mon officier*. The Arabs have spread the news, and the entire garrison is discussing it.'

'You realise the terrible danger which is involved?'

Duparne did. He was not only a veteran soldier, but also an astute one. Monclaire said: 'At any cost, the Arabs must be prevented from taking the labour away from Vateau. They cannot appreciate just what they are proposing to do, or they would not do it. There is only one course open. I'm going to send you and a small detachment of legionnaires to Vateau. With luck you'll get there before the Arabs. Your task will be to dissuade them from this plan.'

Duparne looked thoughtful.

'Willingly, *mon capitaine* . . . but already there are legionnaires there. Could not they — '

Monclaire interrupted. 'They will not be aware of what is happening until it is too late. I shall give you a letter which you will present to the commanding officer, a Lieutenant Raynard. He will give you all assistance. But I'm entrusting the mission to you because of your experience of the Arabs. I think, *mon sergent*, that you may be able to handle them.'

'How many men shall I take?'

'Your purpose is not war — it is diplomacy. A *peloton* from my company ought to be enough.'

He paused heavily before continuing.

'I shall remain here, but I shall not be inactive. I am going to get a message through to Sadazi — a most urgent message. It will be to ask permission to move almost the entire garrison out of this fort.'

Duparne's eyes widened in baffled astonishment.

'Move the garrison out of this fort! *Mon capitaine*, I . . . '

Monclaire waved his hand for silence.

'No, Sergent, I'm not mad — or I believe that I'm not. Think, man — think! An opportunity such as this can never come again. Those Arabs must be organised. They must be led so that when they meet El Dowla they have some chance of success. There is only one way of achieving that. When they attack Haratzo, a strong Legion force must be with them. A mere company is no good, we need far more than that.

'Once I get permission, I'll leave only a skeleton garrison here. All the rest will force-march to Vateau. There, we'll link up with the Arab rebels, and together we'll fight the Bormones in their bastion . . . '

His eyes were alight. He spoke faster and more loudly than usual.

'Of all times, this is the time to take risks. You must hold the Arabs at Vateau until we arrive . . . then, if fortune is with us, the ordinary Arabs and the legionnaires will fight shoulder to shoulder to end the scourge of the Bormones . . . '

Duparne felt himself infected by the

fire in Monclaire's speech. He, too, saw that such a climax could not only end the tyranny of El Dowla. It could bring about a new understanding between the Arabic people and the garrisons of the Legion.

He said slowly: 'I'll do all I can, *mon officier*. I'll leave at once. I take it I may pick my own men?'

'You may . . . is it that you wish to take the American, Legionnaire Regan, with you?' There was a faint and knowing smile on Monclaire's lips. Duparne was smiling too when he answered.

'I'd thought of him. He is — er — not very orthodox as a soldier, and this is an unorthodox task, so he ought to be suitable. Those friends, too . . . the two other Americans and that blond Englishman. They are useful. I'm going to take them all to Vateau.'

11

March to Vateau

Dice was mildly annoyed.

For the first ten minutes since his release from the detention block, he'd held the attention of every legionnaire in the barrack room as he described the events which had followed his dive over the ramparts. Then someone had come in with the announcement that Major Dux was dead — shot himself.

Immediately, they all forgot about Dice, and began eager discussion about Dux. Dice was as interested as any of them, but it was still human to be annoyed. He had not particularly wanted to describe his time in the desert with Monclaire. In fact, it was only to still the incessant questioning that he did so. But, once started, he warmed up to the narrative, and no man likes being interrupted when he is talking about himself. There was only one consolation.

He'd pretty well finished the story.

However, the slight resentment passed as he listened to the conjectures about Major Dux. Certainly the major had never seemed to him to be the type to commit suicide. In most cases, suicide required a measure of guts.

Then a legionnaire came in with a new report. It was an accident, he announced. He'd shot himself while cleaning his pistol. Monclaire was there when it happened. The legionnaire had got the facts from a medical orderly who'd heard it from the medical officer.

That made Dice think fast.

He'd seen the fury on Monclaire's face when he'd been arrested on the orders of Major Dux. Monclaire had not said anything to him then, but his expression had made it clear that he would do plenty on his behalf. Suddenly Dice had an unpleasant, ugly sort of feeling. He'd not worried much during his short time in the detention block, because he was sure that even a fool like Dux would have to listen to Monclaire. But had something happened between them — something serious . . . ?

There was no shred of real evidence to back it, of course, but still Dice had a hunch . . . and those hunches of his weren't often wrong. He almost said something about it to Marleigh, then decided not to. Not yet, anyway. Whatever had happened before Dux died could be no more than justice. He'd tried his worst to murder Monclaire.

The talk was at its height when it ceased as though every man in the company had been struck dumb. It was killed by the addition of a single shrieking voice. A voice which cut into the sense by its incisive power. The voice of Sergeant Duparne.

'*Legionnaires . . . Attention!*'

The momentary silence was broken as more than a hundred pairs of feet came together. The men solidified where they stood, and as most of them were in groups facing each other, they looked faintly ridiculous.

Duparne hitched his cape over his shoulders. He surveyed them with calculated venom.

'What is this? A meeting place for old

161

women? *Ma foi!* Is it that you have nothing better to do than talk? Is it that your equipment is too perfectly clean that you need not bother about it? Is the condition of your rifles such that the commandant would be pleased if he saw them?' He paused in his rhetorical questioning to glance at the uniform tunics, then towards the row of rifles in their stands.

'But I see it is not so. Your clothing is filthy. Your rifles are full of sand. *Gardez bien, mes legionnaires?* You are not here to rest and debate. Forty men are to parade immediately for special duty. They will be in marching order. *Attention!* These are the names . . . '

He read rapidly from a list which he pulled out of a pocket. Dice heard his name with a mixture of surprise and curiosity. So did Marleigh, Glass, and Curls.

When Duparne had left and the forty men were assembling their kit, Glass said to Dice: 'You know, I figure we four've been kept together deliberately. It's too much of a coincidence that we could all

162

have been selected by chance.'

Dice watched Glass inserting his eye into the socket, and said: 'There's more in it than that. I was expecting a move to Vateau, especially as all the Arabs are now after El Dowla's blood. But I thought the whole company would go, not just a few of us. That was what was originally planned. Still, I guess we'll hear what it's all about before long. That's one thing about this man's army — you always get the bad news prompt.'

They got it when they paraded ten minutes later.

Monclaire spoke to them. Dice noticed that the captain seemed to be suffering from the after-effects of severe strain. At first he thought it might be the result of his capture and escape. Then he was sure it was something else. A toughened soldier like Monclaire would not be worried by such events, particularly since their only hardship had been physical, and that had not been prolonged. Looking at the tight-drawn lips, Dice was convinced that it was largely nervous tension which was afflicting Monclaire.

He became convinced of what had happened in Major Dux's office . . .

But soon his mind was fastened onto the significance of Monclaire's words. Like every other legionnaire in the parade, he was fascinated by the description of the Arab revolt and of the danger at Vateau. And he was moved to admiration for Monclaire's lucid appraisement of the situation and his plan to exploit it.

It was early afternoon when the detachment, with Duparne at its head, marched through the great gateway of Fort Ney and eastwards towards the descending sun.

They saw the first of the Arabs on the next day, when they were within a couple of hours' marching time of Vateau.

It may have been because every man in the detachment was weary, and looking for most of the time at the boots of the legionnaire in front. It may have been because they were all thirsty and wondering why they weren't allowed more than two sips of water every thirty minutes. It may have been because they were all cursing the sun and sand . . .

It may have been because they had a lot

on their minds that they did not see those Arabs until they were close.

They were first attracted by the sound of shouting. Then they lifted their sweating heads to see a long train of robed men. There must have been three hundred of them. Most of them were mounted on mules, but some were walking. They were moving so as to fall in directly behind the Legion column.

Dice was immediately reminded of the volunteers who had relieved Fort Ney. These men looked just the same. The same ordinary and normally peaceful men. The same antiquated weapons. And, it seemed, the same hard determination of men who are prepared to die for justice and security.

One group appeared over the northern horizon and another from the south. Both were moving in the direction of Vateau.

Dice said to Marleigh: 'It looks like we're going to be late. The chances are that a lot of them are already at Vateau, and the damage may have been done.'

Marleigh agreed. By now, the detachment was surrounded on three sides by the Arab irregulars. Glass looked critically at their muskets.

'I sure wouldn't like to try any accurate shooting with those,' he said. 'They look like they'd do as much damage to the guy who fires them as to the enemy.'

Dice was not so sure.

'They did plenty damage to the Bormone camp around Fort Ney,' he told him. But Glass was not listening. His attention had been diverted to the scene directly ahead of them.

'Hell,' Glass said. 'So this is Vateau!'

They were all looking now, and there was an involuntary semi-pause in their steps. They were absorbing a spectacle which might have been created in the fevered mind of a delirious man. A fantastic sight which looked as though it could not be real.

In the centre were the partly completed walls of the fort. They rose stark and ugly out of the sand, like the derelict castle of a folktale giant. All around it there were tents. Hundreds of tents. And outside the tents were long rows of still Arab figures stretched on the sand. Each had part of his robes pulled over his face. Above, some vultures were flapping and screeching.

Some distance from the assembly of corpses, the other Arabs were standing in desultory groups. A few legionnaires were moving about among them, and others were on guard around the fort walls.

As they entered the perimeter of the camp, the Arabs looked sullenly at them. The only sound was the crunch of their feet on the sand.

Duparne halted them outside the Legion guard tent. A lieutenant emerged from it. He looked wanly at the detachment. Duparne saluted and handed him an envelope.

'We're from Fort Ney,' he said. 'We're on special duty. It is explained in this message from Capitaine Monclaire.'

The lieutenant said his name was Raynard. He read the message carefully. The hands which held it were shaking slightly. Then he looked up at Duparne.

'You've wasted your time in coming here,' he said. 'You may have wasted your lives, too. This place has been struck by a plague.'

Every legionnaire heard it. The sentence was spoken clearly, with the loud precision of desperation. But it took time for the meaning to become clear. When it did, there was a shiver of horror along the ranks.

Duparne's skin had gone grey as he said: 'Plague? When did this start, *mon officier*?'

'The first deaths were yesterday. Since then, more than fifty have died — that was the last report an hour ago. More will have gone since then.'

Dice felt his throat swell and become completely dry. He knew, they all knew, of the horrors of eastern plague. It struck suddenly and could decimate whole populations. But it mostly occurred in the squalor of the towns, seldom in smaller desert communities.

Duparne asked, 'Have you a doctor here, *mon officier*?'

'*Non*. Only a medical orderly. It was arranged that any cases of serious sickness would go to Fort Ney first, then on to Sadazi. But we cannot cope with this . . .'

'How many legionnaires have died?'

The lieutenant paused before he said: 'That is rather a curious thing about it . . . So far, I have not lost a legionnaire. All the deaths have been among the Arabs.'

Duparne looked as puzzled as the lieutenant.

'It is indeed extraordinary, *mon officier*. Plague does not usually discriminate among victims.'

The officer said: 'I'm not sure of what I ought to do. To save as many of my men as possible, I ought to move them out of this camp. But if I did that, the fort would be unprotected. I have to decide which is the more important — the lives of the legionnaires, or the safety of a half-built fort.'

He passed an unsteady hand across his damp forehead. The men of the detachment watched him in grim silence. Soldiers are quick to recognise when an officer is out of his depth. They recognised the fact now. It was obvious that this young and probably inexperienced lieutenant was completely submerged by the emergency. And he was frightened, too.

Few of the detachment spoke as they pitched camp beyond the eastern walls of the fort. They knew that here they had no leadership. They felt helpless.

Food in the form of weak soup and coffee was sent to them from the field kitchens. When it was eaten, Duparne told them that they would rest for the remainder of the day. Then he called Dice out from the ranks before dismissing the others.

'Your Arabic is better than mine,' he said, 'so you will come with me. You know that I must try to stop these fools from marching on Haratzo, and you will be able to persuade them better than I.'

His attitude was almost conciliatory. It was seldom, if ever, that Dice had heard Duparne speak like this.

'I don't think they'll need a lot of persuading,' Dice said. 'The way things are, I figure they'll all be getting out of here before very long.'

'Then we must stop that too. Captain Monclaire wants them all held and ready to move when he arrives with the garrison.'

Dice's forecast was correct. Some of

the Arab irregulars had already left, seeking safety in the desert from the plague. Others were preparing to go. There was now an atmosphere of activity. The stunned stillness which had been prevalent when the detachment had arrived was gone. Mules and camels were being saddled for a flight from the stricken camp.

For a few minutes they watched the preparations. Then Dice's gaze drifted towards the place where the bodies of the dead were laid out. In the last hour, a long mass grave had been dug. The first of the victims were being lowered into it by some legionnaires while a man intoned a rite of Islam.

Overhead, the vultures were still hovering and diving, as though maddened by the sight.

Dice began by watching idly. Then his brain flashed back to some words of the officer's. He linked those words with the long row of dead Arabs — *all* Arabs. His brain started to work at speed, assembling facts and deducing probabilities from them.

He said to Duparne: 'I'd like to look at the dead.'

Duparne raised his heavy eyebrows.

'Look at them! *Mon Dieu*, is this morbid curiosity? Surely you have seen enough of death to be past that?'

Dice ignored the question.

'I think it might be worthwhile. Perhaps you'll come and look, too?'

Duparne shrugged his shoulders. '*Tres bien*. I do not know what you are thinking about now, Legionnaire, but I can't waste much time at a graveside. However . . . we'll do as you wish.'

Dice had to subdue a sense of revulsion before he could set about his task. Duparne watched him — gloomily at first, then with growing interest. When Dice had examined six of the bodies, Duparne said, 'It is enough. You are right, Legionnaire. Those men did not die of plague, for there are no plague spots on them.

'They must have been poisoned.'

12

'To Haratzo!'

Duparne looked vacantly into the middle distance after he'd finished speaking.

He'd never been very enthusiastic about this mission. Like most men who have spent a lifetime in an army, Duparne did not like breaking with routine. Still, when Monclaire had given the order, he'd had no choice. And, because of his experience of Arabs, he'd felt fairly confident of being able to handle it. But now this . . . It was something altogether beyond his original reckoning. Something which did not fall within the orbit of military emergencies. He was glad he had this American at his side. He'd not been wrong in bringing him.

Because he felt he ought to say something more, Duparne asked: 'But how is it that the legionnaires have not been struck down too?'

'I figure because it's a whole lot more difficult to tamper with army food,' Dice told him. 'It's almost certain that the poison's been introduced by an Arab who is an agent of El Dowla. He'll be finding it easy to slip the stuff into the communal stewpots that the Arabs use. But he wouldn't get far if he tried to operate in a Legion field kitchen.'

Duparne nodded. He said: 'It was natural for them to think it was plague. And they are so frightened of the disease that they would not think of looking for the skin rash. They must all be told the truth immediately — that will stop the flight into the desert.'

Dice's voice rose with urgency as he answered, 'Hell, no! That would solve nothing. The poisonings could still go on, and the Arabs would be as scared as ever. We've got to find who's doing this.'

Duparne was not convinced.

'That may take time. Days, perhaps. Meanwhile, what happens? I'll tell you. The Arabs will forget about their hatred of the Bormones. They'll forget about their wish to destroy them. They will all go back to their villages. And then, *mon legionnaire*, we'll not only have lost a friendly army, but work will have ceased on the fort also.'

Dice knew that there was a lot of force in Duparne's reasoning. But he also remained convinced that, on balance, his own proposal was the better one.

'They'll be just as afraid of the poisoning as they are of plague,' he urged. 'But I agree that we've got to stop them from running out of here. I think there's a way we can do that. Will you let me talk to them, so you'll see what I mean?'

Duparne gave a tight smile.

'It is becoming no more than a formality for you to ask my permission. The answer is — *oui*. But I do not know what you can possibly have in that so-amazing head of yours.'

With Duparne at his side, Dice strode quickly to where most of the Arabs were preparing for their flight. At first they were given no more than passing glances. But the Arabs paused in their tasks and looked with a semblance of interest as Dice climbed onto a mule cart and gestured them to gather round.

None of them moved. There were more than a thousand Arabs there. They all looked curious but remained immobile.

Yet it seemed that they were ready to listen. After a few seconds' hesitation, Dice pitched his voice well forward as he started to speak. It was not an easy task. Although his command of Arabic was good for conversational purposes, this matter of addressing a big audience was entirely different, and more difficult. And he knew, too, that while he could not reveal the entire truth, it would also be fatal to rely on lies. These Arabs set enormous store by the virtue of absolute honesty, and they were quick to sense any attempt to deceive them.

Dice told them that the affliction which had caused the deaths — he deliberately avoided using the word 'plague' — was now known to be only of a temporary nature. There was a good chance of it passing completely by the next day. In any case, if they went back to their villages, they might bring disease and disaster there, and their families might die . . .

176

This made an immediate impact on them. In their panic they had obviously not considered that possibility. They drew closer round the cart and listened intently as Dice continued.

' . . . new and strong Legion forces are coming,' Dice called. 'They will lead you into battle against the Bormones who murdered the innocent people of Karak. Is it not better to wait for them? If you go back now, your children will say it was because you were afraid . . . '

An Arab who had been labouring on the fort pushed his way to the front until he stood directly beneath Dice. He was a powerful young man, and his robes were thrown loosely over the sinews of his body.

'What you say sounds well,' he said to Dice, loudly enough that most of the others could hear. 'But we may not live to greet the men of the Legion. You say that the disease which has afflicted our brothers will soon pass. Yet how can we be sure of that? Many are dead and many more are sick. It does not seem to us that it will pass.'

Dice had expected that someone would

say something of that sort. He was prepared for it. His answer involved a risk. It
meant that they had less than twenty-four
hours in which to trace the person or
persons responsible for poisoning the food.
But it was a risk that had to be taken.

'You can prove it for yourselves,' he
shouted as some of the Arabs murmured
agreement with the young man. 'Wait
until tomorrow when the sun is at its
zenith. If men are still falling ill by that
hour, then leave Vateau. But stay, I beg
you, until then — '

Sweat was oozing down Dice's cheeks
as he surveyed the mass of upturned
faces. At first there was no sound. None
at all. They continued to look at him.
Then, gradually, they dropped their gaze
and a slow mutter of talk spread among
the throng. This was followed by a general
movement. A movement back to the
donkeys and the camels.

Duparne touched his arm.

'You tried so very hard, *mon legionnaire*,' he said. 'But it seems you have
failed. They are still determined to leave
Vateau . . .'

But Dice scarcely heard the last few words. He saw something which made his heart quicken and forced a sob of relief into his throat.

'They are not leaving,' he gasped back. 'They are staying! Look . . . '

The Arabs were loosening the girths and lifting the saddles off their beasts.

* * *

Lieutenant Raynard was now a little less frightened.

Seated behind a trestle table in his tent, he felt a faint glow of something which was akin to confidence as he listened first to Sergeant Duparne and then to the American legionnaire. He wondered why he'd not thought to check the assumption that plague had caused the deaths. Of course, it seemed to be the obvious answer . . . Still, the fact that he had not done so did not improve his standing as an officer.

But somehow he was not very concerned about his standing. He'd almost decided that he'd had quite enough of the

Legion. He'd only entered it because his father had served in it too. Perhaps, when all this was over, he'd see about resigning his commission . . . Meanwhile, he was quite prepared to leave control to this dynamic little sergeant whom Captain Monclaire had sent. And to this shrewd, quick-witted legionnaire too, for he appeared to enjoy the confidence of Duparne, and he certainly knew a great deal about the Arabs and about the habits of El Dowla's men.

'Let me summarise the situation,' Lieutenant Raynard said in a mild effort to demonstrate authority. 'You feel that, because it has been announced that Legion reinforcements are coming, an effort will be made to get the news to El Dowla in Haratzo?'

'*Oui*,' Duparne said. 'There is at least one agent of El Dowla in our midst, and tonight he may attempt to leave the camp. That will be our chance to find how, and by whom, the food is being poisoned. It is already becoming dark, so I suggest, *mon officier*, that every available legionnaire be drawn round the outside of the camp with orders to hold any who try to leave. But let it be done quietly and without fuss, so that our enemies do not know.'

The lieutenant nodded.

'It shall be as you wish, *mon sergent*. You may take control of the operation and arrange the positions in the way you please.'

As they left the tent, Dice smiled.

'That guy'd make a great general,' he said softly. 'He has the sense to leave the work to other people.'

Duparne affected not to hear.

It was when night had finally settled on the desert, when the campfires were flickering into life and the vultures were quiet, that the legionnaires moved silently out of the camp. Their own tents were pitched beyond the eastern perimeter, so they did not need to pass near the Arabs. Nor were they seen as they formed their wide circle, with a gap of little more than fifty yards between each man.

They had all been given a simple order — they were to detain any person trying to leave the camp, but they were not to shoot unless it appeared that he would otherwise get away.

Dice was fairly certain that the attempt would be made from the western side. He came to that conclusion by putting himself into the position of a person who wanted to get secretly out of Vateau.

Normally the most lightly-guarded side was at the west, for there was least danger from there. Haratzo and the Bormone country were to the east. Also, the western perimeter housed the crude paddocks where the horses were tethered. Therefore Dice, with Duparne's permission, went to that sector.

Every legionnaire lay flat on his stomach, looking inwards towards Vateau. In this way they were practically invisible, yet kept the entire camp under watch.

It gave Dice a pleasant feeling to note that the man on his immediate left was Glass. If trouble came that way, then Glass was a good man to have around. He would have liked Marleigh and Curls to be in the vicinity, too. But it chanced that they were on the northern side, some hundreds of yards distant.

Waiting and doing absolutely nothing

in the dark except watch is an exhausting business. And it can be uncomfortable if you are lying full-length on hard, rocky sand. After the first hour, every grain seems to be biting into your bare flesh. And, following the heat of the day, the air is cold. First it tires you, so that you want to sleep. Then it starts you shivering so that you wake out of a momentary doze.

Gradually, Dice felt his morale sink lower as the hours dragged slowly past. He watched the Arab fires die out one by one, and he longed to feel their warmth. His spirits were not improved by the knowledge that every other legionnaire must be feeling exactly the same — or maybe even worse. It meant that the longer they were there, the less alert they became. And alertness was vital.

It was some time after midnight when the waiting ended.

Dice got his first warning when he heard a distant whinny from the paddock. It was the sort of sound a horse makes when it is awakened out of sleep and hauled to its feet. A sound of impotent protest against the entire race of man.

For minutes after that, there was nothing more to be heard. But Dice had suddenly forgotten his physical discomfort. He was watching — watching into the blackness, his nerves straining.

That which he'd been waiting and hoping to see appeared with only the smallest of warnings.

First he heard the very soft tread of hooves on the sand; then, it seemed, only seconds later, the shadowed form of a man walking at the side of a horse appeared directly ahead of him, no more than twenty yards off. Dice tried to jump to his feet. It was here that he appreciated too late a sheer fact of nature. He appreciated that you cannot lie motionless in the cold for hours on end and then expect your muscles to answer a sudden call to action.

He'd intended to run towards the man, covering him with his rifle. Instead, he got onto one knee, then almost fell flat again as a spasm of cramp shot through his thighs. Trying to ignore the pain, he forced himself up and swayed unsteadily. Then he tried to move towards the robed silhouette. But he could do no more than stumble.

The Arab had seen him long before this. He stood for a moment, as though hesitating. Then, leaving the horse, he turned and ran back towards the camp.

In another couple of seconds he would have been invisible in the darkness. He would have merged again among the hive of Arabs at Vateau, with no hope of finding him. He would have done that if Glass had not been on Dice's left — and if Glass had not been the fastest and most accurate rifle shot in the Legion.

Glass saw exactly what had happened. He did not attempt to rise. As he peeped with his one good eye through the sights of his Lebel, he said to himself: 'I mustn't kill him. I've just got to wing him . . . '

That was exactly what Glass did. There was a stab of fire from the muzzle of the Lebel, a whip-like crack, and a bullet had skimmed through the outer flesh of the Arab's shoulder. It was no more than a superficial wound. But it knocked him off-balance and he fell forwards. By this time, the blood was circulating again through Dice's legs. He was able to run towards the flapping heap of robes. However, when ten yards still separated them, the Arab was again up and running to the camp.

At first he was able to cover the ground faster than Dice. The remnants of the cramp were still restricting Dice's speed, and so was the fact that he was carrying a rifle and equipment. But when the Arab was level with the first of the camp tents, Dice knew that he'd started to gain on him. The Arab knew it too. His next move came with cat-like suddenness.

He swerved slightly, then stopped and turned. A short Bormone knife was in his right hand.

Dice felt the man's warm breath in his face and saw the faint glint of the blade as it started to descend towards his neck. It was his own impetus that saved him. He was moving too fast for the Arab. They crashed together, and the knife did no more than slice the back of his tunic.

Both fell to the ground under the impact. Dice rolled back towards the Arab, his right fist drawn back. It was a lucky punch that he landed. It glanced across the point of the jawbone. The fellow gave out a grunt and was still.

By this time the commotion had been heard. All around, the Arabs were emerging from their tents. Several legionnaires arrived, and so did Duparne. When the man's eyes blinked open, he gazed with a black venom at the chattering mob. Dice gripped his wrists and pulled him to his feet.

He pulled the turban off his face. It revealed the thin, hawk-like features which Dice had expected to see. Not the features one usually found among the village Arabs. That was the face of a killer — the face of a Bormone.

A legionnaire held his arms behind his back while Dice ripped away the robes. He felt through them carefully. Inside a top hem, he felt a series of small bulges. After pulling the stitching away, a half-dozen stone phials fell into his hand. Dice pulled the stopper out of one of them and held the container to his nostrils. Then he passed it to Duparne.

He said: 'Take a whiff of this. I'll lay my

last sou that that's Miyana essence.'

Duparne carefully reinserted the stopper.

'I'm not sure,' he said gravely. 'I know that Miyana is one of the most powerful poisons of the east, but, *ma foi*, I've never before had cause to deal with it. Are you sure, *mon legionnaire*?'

'Almost sure. In weak solutions it is sometimes used for killing insects in the cafés. That's how I recognise the smell. But one of these phials in a bowl of food would kill off a dozen men — particularly as the stuff's almost tasteless.'

The listening Arabs had caught on to his words. They were repeating the name 'Miyana' in awed whispers. But they were whispers which contained a strange undercurrent.

Dice went on: 'We can soon find out if I'm right. We can ask this man to taste a little of it.' He indicated the Arab in the now-torn robes. Slowly, Dice extended a phial towards the man's tight-clenched lips. The Arab's eyes dilated and he turned away his head. Dice glanced at a legionnaire. 'Force open his mouth,' he ordered. 'Do it by gripping his nostrils.'

As the legionnaire's fingers closed over the nose, the man gave out a whimpering scream. It was followed by a tornado of words. Words which admitted that the liquid was Miyana, admitted that he'd inserted it in the food . . . pleaded that he be not forced to take it.

The Bormone's nerve had gone. He'd given way to wild, gabbling hysteria. But this was drowned by a new sound. It came from the Arabs. It came as they realised why so many had died — and who had caused them to die. They started to press round the Bormone. Deadly intentions are usually obvious. Duparne shouted an order, and the legionnaires attempted to make a protecting ring round the man. He might still have information of value. They did not want him to die — yet.

But it was too late. The legionnaires were torn aside under a quick rush of bodies. There was a swirling of robes, the sound of deep and noisy breathing. When at last the Arabs were dragged away, they left a messy and huddled human remnant on the ground. The Bormone had been ripped to death as though by some ferocious animal. And then a new cry went up from the Arabs. A cry which swept like a blaze across the entire camp. Their voices called: '*To Haratzo . . . to Haratzo . . . death to the men of El Dowla!*'

13

The Last Battle

It was as though they had forgotten how to sleep. As though the lust for vengeance had dominated every other facet of their minds. For throughout the remainder of the night, the Arabs continued the chanting. Only when the dawn came did they cease. And even then they did not rest. Despite the appeals of Duparne, despite an attempt to reason with them by Dice, they started to move away from Vateau. And their objective was Haratzo.

It was after he had watched them streaming eastwards across the desert that Duparne entered the tent of Lieutenant Raynard. The sergeant's salute was little more than an upward gesture of the hand. He did not wait for permission to speak.

'*Mon officier*, we must move on Haratzo with the Arabs. There is no time to wait for Capitaine Monclaire's force. You have a few hundred men here. Together we ought to be able to hold the Bormones until the others arrive.'

Lieutenant Raynard looked at him with disapproving astonishment.

'You suggest that I should denude the new fort of all protection. This is preposterous!'

'It is of little use at the moment, *mon officier*, for no one is working on it. They have all left for Haratzo. Don't you see that if we let those Arabs attack on their own, they'll be cut down *en masse*? Their power will be lost to us forever. I know that the risk is terrible, but we must take it.'

Raynard leaned forward and almost uptilted his trestle table.

'Must take it! Are you giving me orders? Be careful, Sergent. You have been allowed latitude because of the special duties which Capitaine Monclaire gave to you. But we have not yet reached the stage at which N.C.O.s command a camp.'

Beneath his deep tan, Duparne flushed at the thinly disguised jibe. He said sharply: 'Then I shall take my own forty men. They are under my direct command and you cannot interfere.'

Lieutenant Raynard pulled a sweat rag out of his pocket. He dabbed his face before answering. 'You're being a fool. Do you realise that El Dowla has far more warriors mobilised than ever before? If those Arabs are intent on being massacred by them, then it's their affair. But that you should think of taking your own paltry detachment with them so as to share their fate . . . it is madness.'

'I don't think of it as madness, *mon officier*. It is my duty. I've tried to hold them back, but such is their fury at the poisonings that they will not listen. So I must march with them. Even my forty men may make it possible for them to hold on until Capitaine Monclaire reaches us.'

Raynard dabbed again with the rag. The tremble was back again in his hands.

'Then you're hoping for a miracle. Neither your men nor the Arabs will last ten minutes against the Bormones. And remember, Monclaire may not even get permission to move the garrison. It is an unprecedented proposal to leave a fort with only a skeleton guard. I've decided . . . '

No one ever knew what it was that Raynard had decided. His words faded and were lost beneath the ragged explosions from many muskets. Duparne wheeled towards the tent opening, and in doing so nearly collided with Dux's orderly, who rushed in. The corporal had been running hard. He was sucking in his breath to an accompaniment of wild gasps. Streaming sweat from his forehead was smarting in his eyes.

'*Mon officier* . . . the Bormones are approaching . . . many thousands of them . . . '

There was a brief period in which both Duparne and Raynard appeared to be paralysed. During it, each watched the corporal without making any suggestion of movement. Then, very slowly, Duparne turned again to the lieutenant.

'It seems our differences are over,' he said dryly.

He strode out of the tent, Raynard following.

The oasis of Vateau was on the apex of a slight slope. Until they began to build the fort there, it was no more than a little-used watering place. Other oases in the vicinity were better placed across the caravan trade routes, and therefore more popular.

Now the half-built walls of the fort enclosed the subterranean well, and the place was a sprawling mass of habitation. But the tactical view remained the same. Immediately Duparne and Raynard emerged from the tent, they were able to see miles into the surrounding desert.

On three sides the sand rolled and glinted under a brassy sun, bare of any suggestion of life. But not on the other side. On the east side it was different.

The lines of the Bormone armies were two miles away. The depth of the ranks could be counted in scores, and from end to end they stretched over a distance of fully a thousand yards. On the flanks were the cavalry, the riders keeping slow pace with the massed foot warriors in the centre.

The white robes, their red edgings just

visible, were like the massive crest of some irresistible wave — a wave which, it seemed, in the certainty of time would engulf and destroy Vateau. The warriors of El Dowla were moving with a precision which was born of discipline.

That discipline was in harsh contrast to the spectacle presented by the Arab irregulars.

Appalled by the strength which had suddenly and unexpectedly come upon them so soon after leaving Vateau, they were streaming back towards the camp. There had been only a momentary attempt at a stand, and that had lasted only long enough for a few hundred of them to discharge that futile volley.

It was not that they lacked courage, or even that their normal courage had deserted them. They fled aghast because they had never imagined that any man — even El Dowla — could move against them such array as this. Most of them had not previously seen a fighting force of greater size than a Legion company. This spectacle twisted and abducted their untutored imaginations.

In any case, none but the crazed would have remained in the open to resist such a force. It would be like trying to repel a sandstorm by blowing with one's mouth. In chattering and cursing chaos, they fled back to the friendly camp of Vateau: the camp which was protected by the rifles of the Legion.

Again, Duparne and Raynard wasted time. They wasted priceless minutes gazing with horror on the scene. It was a scene which, through the scale of its foreboding, numbed the imagination and rocked the judgment.

Duparne was the first to get a grip on his senses.

He said: 'We must fall back within the fort, walls, *mon officier.*'

Raynard dragged his eyes towards Duparne. They held a new and desperate light.

'What's the use of that? At best, the walls are only half-built, and in some places they're up only a few feet . . . *mon sergent*, this is certain death, so we might as well meet it out here like men and let it be over quickly.'

Duparne glanced curiously at him. Raynard certainly had severe limitations as a tactician, and even as an administrator. But his words suggested that there could be no doubt of his physical courage.

'With respect, that would be wrong, *mon officier*. It is clearly our duty to sell our lives as dearly as we can. Those walls at least give some cover. With every Arab and every legionnaire behind them, we may be able to hold out for hours.'

Raynard hesitated. He'd been in the grip of a suicidal urge for battle soon, and at any cost — the sort of primitive emotion which can seize men when faced with impossible and deadly odds. But now the urge had subsided. He nodded.

'Very well. Get everyone behind the walls.'

Perhaps, if he'd been granted a more fortunate turn of his wheel of fate, Duparne would not have been an N.C.O. If those unfathomed forces which direct human fortune had been a little more beneficent, he might have yet been a soldier of distinguished rank. For in such moments as this, moments when survival depended on clear thinking blended with innate military instinct, Duparne was at his brilliant best.

Within minutes, he had parties of legionnaires posted all around the camp, directing the retreating Arabs inside the walls.

In a further few minutes, he'd organised more legionnaires to move food and ammunition out of the tents and into the cover of the fort.

It could have been that deep, very deep, within him, Sergeant Duparne was enjoying it all. Perhaps he was obtaining some grim pleasure out of this climax to a lifetime spent in the study and the service of arms. This was his greatest test. He was calling upon all his skill and knowledge to meet it.

His improvised organisation worked without a hitch. But when the last of the Arabs were within the walls and the three hundred legionnaires had taken up their positions, then the shell of Fort Vateau was seriously overcrowded. Arabs and legionnaires alternated at defence positions behind those walls. Where the walls were high, they had piled up packing cases so as to form firing platforms. Where they were low, the men crouched or stood. And there was no more than a foot of space between each man.

Behind, in the square, the remaining Arabs were standing in strained silence. It was impossible to accurately estimate their numbers, but they must have totalled well over a thousand, for the big space was so full that none could move freely.

This meant that in the event of a Bormone break-in they would scarcely be able to defend themselves.

And there was another weakness . . . the wide gap wherein the fort gates were to be placed. Four ranks of legionnaires and Arabs guarded this.

Dice had taken up a position where the wall was only five feet high. This offered a good upright firing stance. He saw that Duparne, his pistol out, was quite near to him. So was Raynard. He caught a glimpse of Marleigh and Curls. They were at a high sector of the wall. Glass was placed a little beyond them: Dice saw him rest his Lebel between two long Arab muskets.

At first, the Bormones stood off from the camp as though suspicious of the quiet. Then Dice heard a legionnaire whisper, 'They're coming in!' Immediately afterwards, he discerned the faint clink of bridles. Then he saw the cavalry encircling and entering the outer perimeter. Gradually, they came more fully into view, guiding their horses between the tents and towards the fort.

As he watched them, Dice could not entirely subdue a feeling of grudging admiration.

These were amongst the most cruel warriors in the east. The lost women and children of Karak bore testimony to the fact that they were utterly without mercy. Yet . . . with their robes billowing slightly and their demeanour of contemptuous confidence, they presented a magnificent picture of brutal but disciplined force.

The cavalry halted when they were four hundred yards from the wall. They waited for the foot warriors to draw up behind them. Their plan was obvious. It was intended that the cavalry should charge the low sections of the wall, using the weight of their animals to force back the defenders. The others would follow through the gaps with their knives and scimitars . . .

This was bound to result in great casualties to the Bormones — but what did great casualties matter to so many?

The attack did not come immediately. The cavalry and the foot warriors remained still, looking at the walls. The delay puzzled legionnaires and Arabs alike. They nervously fingered rifle and musket.

Those with Dice on the west side were the first to know the reason. It came in the form of one hundred additional cavalry, each astride a superb white steed. The riders wore robes of white and purple silk, and their saddles were brocaded in gold. Dice knew who they were. Dice had seen them before.

This was the elite corps of the Bormones. This was El Dowla's personal guard.

And at the head of them was El Dowla.

The shafts from the sun played upon the great emerald in his turban. They glittered off the gemmed rings which hung from his fingers. They seemed to play lovingly on the richness of his all-purple robes — robes which accentuated the grossness of the man.

Yet there could be no doubt of the effect he was having upon his armies. Even from behind the walls, the legionnaires and Arabs could sense the hushed wonder which greeted his arrival. Among the Bormones, El Dowla was indeed a living legend. Their dreams of conquest were based upon his foresight, cunning and inspiration.

Without any warning, Dice felt a constriction inside his chest. It made breathing unpleasant. There was a slight ache in his head, too. At first he could not understand it. Then he knew the reason.

His mind and his body were being gripped by his hatred of the leader of the Bormones. It was a hatred, long held in check, which now threatened to take an absolute hold on him.

El Dowla . . . he was looking at him

. . . looking at the man who had murdered his brother . . . the man who had ordered the slaying of the weak and the helpless in Karak . . . who had hypnotised thousands of his followers into accepting and believing in his plans for crazy conquest. But most of all . . . most of all . . . Dice hated him for what had been done to that innocent American . . . to his brother.

It was only dimly that Dice was aware of the Bormone preparations for attack. Always, his eyes were watching the fat, purple-clad figure who sat his horse at the head of his guard, a little distance behind the ordinary cavalry.

Dice was realising that above and beyond all else, he must try to kill El Dowla that day. Once before, he'd tried and failed. There must be no failure this time. An opportunity must present itself. In his confidence, the man might move within range of his rifle. Just one bullet in that fat flesh, then Dice Regan would willingly share the fate of all the others who manned the walls. For the capture of Vateau, the end of the prospect of a

Legion fort there, would avail the Bormones nothing if they lost the leadership of El Dowla.

Dice dragged a limp hand across his forehead. The intensity of his emotion had made him feel temporarily weak. He whispered to himself: 'Hell ... I never knew I could hate like this ... '

The Bormone cavalry attacked.

The advance was conducted, like all Bormone battle operations, with skill and imagination. In relation to the number of men available, they had only a small object to attack. They did not make the mistake of trying to concentrate too many horseman into the first wave, thus risking crowding and confusion. It seemed that no more than one in every five moved out from the lines and bore down on the walls.

But even that was a considerable number — certainly more than a thousand.

At first they did no more than trot towards the walls. Their scimitars were held upright against their shoulders. It was when they were three hundred yards off and getting within accurate small-arms range that they lowered their blades so that they extended over the heads of their mounts. Their bodies, too, rose and leaned forward in the saddles. And the horses broke into a full gallop.

The Bormone cavalry were charging.

Orders had been given to the Arabs to withhold their fire until the legionnaires opened up. That order had been given by Duparne, but without much confidence that it would be obeyed. His pessimism was well justified.

As soon as the gallop began there was a weak rattle of musketry from the Arabs. Some of their ammunition was so poor that, even at that decreasing range, a fair number of shots fell short and spent in the sand. Very few of the others hit a target. Certainly, so far as Dice could see, none of the Bormones was brought down.

The legionnaires waited for the blast from the whistle which Duparne held between his teeth. Duparne, in turn, was waiting for a hand signal from Lieutenant Raynard. Under the stress of physical action Raynard was no longer vacillating, no longer incompetent. Other types of emergencies had defeated him. They were emergencies calling for diplomacy and foresight. But this one did not worry him. This, he could understand.

When the Bormones were within fifty yards of the walls, Raynard brought down his upraised right hand. In the same second the peal of the whistle was heard above the thud of hooves, above the spasmodic fire of the muskets.

Three hundred Lebels nudged back against the shoulders of the men who gripped them. Three hundred cylinders of lead with a muzzle velocity of a mile in every three seconds screamed through space in the direction of the Bormones. In that first volley, almost every shot seemed to find a mark. Where riders were not hit, the horses stumbled and went down. Great and ugly gaps were torn in the attacking ranks.

There followed the briefest moment of comparative quiet in which the only sound was the click of bolts being drawn back then pushed forward again. Then for a second time the hot air was tortured and torn under the exploding crash of compressed cordite.

But this time the effect was not so great. The legionnaires had not had time to aim, for the cavalry were now very close. Some were no more than twenty yards from the walls.

And they were turning so as to converge on the lower sectors where the horses could jump into the fort.

After he'd fired the second round, Dice's right hand automatically tried to pull back the bolt. But it would not move.

Cursing, he pulled upwards again with all his strength. Still the bolt remained fixed. He swore again and looked desperately around. He knew that nothing could be done with his rifle. This was a serious stoppage, probably caused by a split cartridge casing which had expanded and seized in the magazine. Only an armourer would be able to get it out.

So far, but only so far, there had been no casualties among the legionnaires. There was no spare weapon which he could use. Then he looked again towards the Bormones. And what he saw drove his feeling of helplessness from his mind. He saw El Dowla. And El Dowla was very near to his part of the walls.

Slightly ahead of his guard, he had moved up to a position within thirty yards of Dice and directly behind his cavalry. Physical cowardice was certainly not among El Dowla's sins, and by this action he probably hoped to inspire his men further. But he was not apparently in very great danger. He was shielded from the direct line of fire by his attacking horsemen. His only risk was that of a chance shot.

Dice did not know whether he came to any decision to break out of the fort. Certainly he was not aware of thinking about it. It must have been some mad instinctive action which made him leap over the low stonework at the moment a Bormone horseman was gathering his steed for a jump into the fort.

Seeing Dice, the Bormone attempted to rein his horse aside. But he was too late. Pulled off balance and in the middle of a jumping stride, the animal crashed against the low parapet, throwing its rider inside the fort.

Dice was no more than dimly aware of this. He knew that he was now standing outside the comparative sanctuary of the walls. He knew that there was nothing between him and the cavalry. But he also knew that just beyond those warriors was El Dowla. He glimpsed him as a splash of purple . . .

The legionnaires had not yet fixed bayonets. That operation would take place at the last critical moment, for bayonets seriously upset the accuracy of rifle fire. Dice's bayonet was in its scabbard. He drew it out. Now he had a weapon . . . a weapon with which to kill . . . to kill El Dowla.

A couple of horsemen seemed to be charging directly at him. The noise from the hooves shook his eardrums, and he saw every detail of the hard faces of their riders. But they swept past, intent on the low area of wall. In the fury and the carnage they had not seen the single legionnaire. And if they had, they probably would not have bothered about him. He was unarmed. He could wait.

Dice felt a rush of air and a sound like

the plucking of high-tension strings as he started to move forward. It was another volley from the legionnaires. The bullets which passed his head brought down several of the Bormones directly in front. For a moment — just for this moment, perhaps — there was no one between him and El Dowla.

There did not seem to be any interval of time between the second when he saw him and that in which he was directly under the saddle of the Bormone chief's white charger. He saw El Dowla turn and look down at him. Saw, too, the expression of astonishment on his fleshy face. Then Dice's bayonet stabbed forward. There seemed to be practically no resistance to the steel as it penetrated those purple robes then entered the massive body.

Vaguely, Dice saw the blood ooze out and blend with the robes. Then El Dowla rolled sideways out of the saddle. He was dead when he dropped at Dice's feet.

It was curious, but Dice felt no sense of triumph, no exultation. Rather did the primitive sense of self-preservation return to him. With the reddened blade in his hand, he looked towards El Dowla's personal guard, wondering if anything, anything at all, could be done before they had a chance to cut him down. It was only the fact that El Dowla had placed himself some little way ahead of his elite corps which had enabled Dice to reach him.

But at first the guard did not move. Drawn up in a compact square, they stood as though cast out of wax. To them, this was a facet of time in which neither brain nor flesh would work. They had seen their leader die. Die without warning as though at the hands of some mad devil. El Dowla stabbed to death ... stabbed like any mortal man. He, whom it was said none could kill. He who was almost immortal among mortal men ...

This was the finale, the utterly unexpected catastrophe. It took time for their minds to recover from it.

But they did recover. The guard started to move on Dice.

And at that second Dice became aware

of two distinct happenings.

One was that all around him he heard voices, voices in the Bormone dialect, screaming the fact that El Dowla had died. And as they screamed they moved away from the walls, no longer looking like warriors . . . Rather did they look like defeated men.

The other was the emergence through the din of a new tornado of sound. The sound of Lebels. But different Lebels. Many hundreds of them, and from a position outside the fort walls and to the south of them. The Bormones appeared to fall as though cut with a satanic scythe. One of those Lebel bullets cut into Dice's shoulder. He felt it lodge, hot and agonising, somewhere in his chest. Before he collapsed, he caught a distant glimpse of Captain Monclaire's garrison. They were firing after the retreating Bormones.

★ ★ ★

Today, if you are fortunate enough to get a permit from the Legion headquarters in Algiers, you can go to the oasis of Vateau.

There you will be able to see the walls behind which the legionnaires fought. Empty ammunition boxes and expended cartridge cases are still scattered on the ground. You might, if some stray Arab has not purloined it, find a Lebel rifle with a jammed breech bolt.

For the fort was never finished. There was no need to finish it. Not when the whole of Morocco shook at the news of El Dowla's death, and of the rout of the Bormone armies. The Bormones still say it was the will of Allah. It was never intended that their people should dominate the vast sweeps of the desert. And now they live in peace, giving little or no trouble to the Legion outpost at Fort Ney.

The Arabs in the villages live in peace, too. But the children outside the hovels listen and wonder as their fathers tell them of the day when they fought side by side with the Legion for the liberation of their lands.

Captain Monclaire? Yes, he still serves in Morocco, but he is a major now. Duparne is still with the Legion — as a warrant officer.

Dice Regan? You would have to cross the Atlantic to find him. Yes, he's back home, and he has a relic of his Legion service. It is a bullet scar behind his left shoulder. A little time ago, Marleigh came over from England to visit him. Glass and Curls were there, too. They wanted to talk about the days when they served in the desert. But they did not have much opportunity to do that. Most of the time they were compelled to listen.

They had to listen to Curls telling them about the time he was in the ring with Joe Louis.

Other titles in the
Linford Mystery Library:

COLD CALLING

Geraldine Ryan

Pronounced unfit for frontline duty due to injury, and eligible to retire in a year, DS Fran Phoenix is given a new job heading up the cold cases team — or 'put in a corner' in the basement, as she sees it. Teamed up with a PC with barely two years' experience, they reopen the twenty-five-year-old case of a missing girl — but evidence continues to be thin on the ground. Can the oddly matched duo heat up the trail and uncover the truth? Three stories from the pen of Geraldine Ryan.

LORD JAMES HARRINGTON AND THE CORNISH MYSTERY

Lynn Florkiewicz

While on holiday with his wife Beth in Cornwall, James learns that a local fisherman vanished during the recent opening procession of the Cornish Legends Festival. When more men disappear in broad daylight, he can't help but put his sleuthing hat on. If they were kidnapped, why is there no ransom demand? What are the flashing lights off the coastline? Who is the eccentric woman on the moors? Have the Cornish Legends really come to life? As James delves into the mystery, he realizes his questions come at a price . . .